The Christ Conspiracy

by
Jack Michael

II

Scripture quotations in this book, unless otherwise noted, are from, "The New King James Version. Copyright© 1979, 1980, 1982, Thomas Nelson Inc., Publishers."

The Christ Conspiracy
ISBN 0-9629844-3-4

Copyright© 1994
by Jack Michael

Jack Michael Outreach Ministries
P.O. Box 10688
Winston-Salem, N.C. 27108-0688

The main characters, places and events in this book are fictional. Although the book occasionally refers to actual people, places or events, the overall intent remains fictional in nature. Other similarities to actual people, places or events is coincidental.

Printed in the United States of America. All rights reserved under International Copyright Law. Contents and/or cover may not be reproduced in whole or in part in any form without the express written consent of the publisher.

IV

I would like to dedicate
this book to my mother:

June Hastings Michael,

who I can truthfully say,
ALWAYS ENCOURAGED ME!

VI

Introduction

What kind of child could potentially grow up to become a dangerous cult leader?

Would parental training, or a lack of it, be a factor in shaping his future?

Would he be a strong-willed child who never received proper discipline; and therefore grew up rebellious, always demanding to have his own way?

Or, would he perhaps be an insecure child who never received encouragement or acceptance; and was therefore too easily influenced by the wrong people?

Would he be a young man who, entirely on his own, thought up fanciful beliefs or strange doctrines?

Or, would he himself be tricked and deluded due, perhaps, to the intrusion of a deceiving spirit?

Maybe he would be a combination of many damaging character flaws!

Regardless of whatever factors shape the lives of future cult leaders, Jesus plainly warns us in his word that many such people will characterize the end times.

In Matthew, chapter 24, the disciples once asked Jesus, *"....what will be the sign of Your coming, and of the end of the age?"*

The answer Jesus gave, more and more reflects the spiritual climate of our world, *"....take heed that no one deceives you. For many will come in My name, saying, I am the Christ, and will deceive many!"*

A few words of explanation. When Jesus said, *"....many will come in My name, saying, I AM THE CHRIST....,"* he wasn't necessarily saying that people would claim to be Jesus Christ of Nazareth, the son of Mary, of the house and lineage of David.

The word *"Christ"* is not a last name. It's a title, which literally means: *"anointed or messiah."* Also, the word *"messiah,"* although often attributed to the Lord Jesus Christ; can simply mean, *"the professed or accepted leader of some hope or cause."*

The many false christs which will characterize these end times, will essentially be saying, *"I am the anointed one, I am the messiah, I am the one you have been looking for;"* while at the same time, suggesting that *"Jesus, the Christ"* was insufficient as the Messiah!

Go with me now into a fictional setting; which although written primarily to provide interesting and exciting reading; could also provide you with wisdom which may someday save your very life from destruction!

The Christ Conspiracy

x

Book One

Foundations

"If the foundations are destroyed, what can the righteous do?"

> The Psalmist David
> Psalm 11, verse 3

Chapter One

Bradley Eugene Hawkins' birth was rather uneventful. Belinda Sue's mother, Nellie stayed with her during the delivery. Her older sister, Pearl, and big brother, Frank dropped by the hospital for short, and rather curt visits, but that was about it. The whole matter was somewhat of an embarrassment to the family. Bradley was born out of wedlock!

Anything, and almost everything that happened in this sleepy, little, west Texas town of Cartersville, was beyond privacy, much less secrecy.

Consequently, the entire town population; officially listed at the somewhat inflated figure of 1,200; knew all about Belinda Sue Hawkins' predicament.

Belinda Sue had dropped out of high school at the age of 16. She didn't have very much going for her in the way of job skills.

There wasn't much work available in Cartersville anyway. Since the mill moved to the more profitable area of Fort Worth, Cartersville had become basically a pit stop for the many transfer trucks rolling up and down the highways.

However, there was one thing Belinda Sue definitely had going for her. She was very pretty! Long blonde hair, tall, slim and shapely, and a bouncy way about her. Consequently, she was quickly hired as a waitress down at Low Boy's Truck Stop.

Low Boy was an interesting fellow. He was barely five feet tall, if that; and a little on the pudgy side. He was balding on top, but had a well coiffured goatee; and always, a foul smelling cigar in his mouth.

Although it was never publicly admitted, It was nonetheless a well known fact that Low Boy didn't hire just waitresses. The hundreds of truckers, cowboys, so-called businessmen, and various other *"rebel rousers"* stopped there for one purpose, the girls!

Nellie halfheartedly cautioned Belinda Sue about this potentially promiscuous lifestyle. For the most part, these cautions went unheeded, because Nellie wasn't all that great a role model herself.

Belinda Sue barely knew her dad. He was also a trucker, and had run off with some strange woman when she was small. Since that time, she had experienced a number of men sojourning through their home.

As expected, she was an overnight success at Low Boy's. With her perky manner and long blonde hair bouncing about, she was in constant demand.

Her life quickly fell into the pattern of part-time waitress and full-time prostitute. By the time she was 19, she had slept with more men than she cared to remember. It was amazing that she hadn't gotten pregnant before now!

So, this was Bradley Eugene Hawkins' entrance into the world. His birth certificate didn't bear the name of a father. It could have been any of four men during the period of time when Belinda Sue realized she was pregnant.

Even if somehow, she could pinpoint who the father was, she probably wouldn't remember his name; and it was unlikely that she would ever see him again.

Nevertheless, shortly after giving birth, She was back working at Low Boy's, justifying her lifestyle of prostitution, because, *"after all, it takes money to raise a family these days!"*

Consequently, young Bradley didn't see very much of his mom. She was always working until the early hours of the morning, and then sleeping away half the day.

The responsibility for child rearing was left primarily in the hands of Grandma Nell, who really didn't have much of a heart for the task!

Secretly, from the depths of her heart, Belinda Sue wished, waited and fantasized about that special man who was somehow mysteriously going to come along, and deliver her from this empty lifestyle.

Unfortunately, he never came!

Chapter Two

From an infant, it was apparent that Bradley was a bright child. The town's people jokingly said that he was smarter than Belinda Sue and Grandma Nell put together. But, there was a serious problem brewing. Bradley received very little supervision, and even less discipline.

Consequently, he quickly learned to use his cleverness to manipulate his mom and grandmother. One way or another, whether through his budding intelligence or through temper tantrums, Bradley got his way. To put it simply, he was pretty much in control of the home!

And, this capability to manipulate people and gain control wasn't just limited to home. He especially learned to seize control of situations if there were other children involved.

For example, there was the Christmas when Bradley was 10 years old. The family had gathered together at Uncle Frank's for their annual Christmas dinner and holiday celebration.

Bradley had three cousins. First, there was Glenda, Aunt Pearl's daughter, who was seven months younger than he. Then, Uncle Frank had two sons, Richard and Timothy, who were 12 and 9 respectively.

As the adults reminisced about Christmases past over a pot of hot Russian Tea and Moravian Sugar Cake; Bradley took advantage of the circumstances to plot a mischievous scheme.

Finding an isolated part of the house, he secretly gathered Glenda, Richard and Timothy together with an air of great importance and anticipation!

He had acquired some old Mexican coins, which at face value were worth very little. But, he made it seem like they were of great value; like prized possessions to be gained at any cost.

He then devised a plan whereby each of his cousins could be rewarded with a portion of the coins. First, however, they must fulfill a daring task.

Richard, the oldest was required to sneak into his parent's bedroom and retrieve a bullet from the pistol his father kept on the top shelf of his closet.

Nine year old Timothy was required to obtain a *"shot glass"* of whiskey, almost from under the noses of the adults, bring it back to the cousins rendezvous, and drink it in one gulp.

Glenda's assignment was easier, just more degrading. She was simply required to remove all of her clothes in front of the other cousins.

As each cousin fulfilled their daring task, Bradley doled out the seemingly important coins into their eagerly waiting hands.

It so happened that Bradley's game was uncovered by Uncle Frank. Pearl exploded at Belinda Sue, *"if you want to take off your clothes and parade yourself naked in front of strange men, that's your business, but I can assure you that my daughter will be brought up with considerably more decency and dignity."*

So much for that year's Christmas celebration!

Uncle Frank insisted that Bradley be punished. Belinda Sue and Grandma Nell made a halfhearted attempt at scolding him; but both made excuses, emphasizing that, *"boys will be boys, and anyway, no real harm was done."*

Deep down, Belinda Sue chuckled to herself. In a way, she sort of admired Bradley's ingenuity.

As for Bradley, he wasn't trying to start Richard on a life of crime. He wasn't interested in turning Tim into a young alcoholic. Neither was he yet interested in the difference of Glenda's anatomy. What Bradley was after was control. This was just another successful, manipulative ploy.

And, so went Bradley Hawkins' childhood. Without proper parental supervision, training, and especially discipline, he was actually a child out of control, rather than in control as he imagined!

"The rod and reproof give wisdom, but a child left to himself brings shame to his mother."

The Wisdom of King Solomon
Proverbs, Chapter 29, verse 15

Chapter Three

Oddly enough, Bradley was always an excellent student. Not that he cared about academics. He was just determined that he would not be outdone by any other student.

He was the only kid in Cartersville Elementary School without a father. This fact resulted in much teasing, which angered him and made him even more determined to be at the head of the class.

Of course, being at the head of the class put him into a position of great favor with his teachers. Ultimately, this just provided him with more opportunities to manipulate situations and have his way.

Despite his spoiled and undisciplined personality, Bradley's academic accomplishments pleased his teachers. From first grade through high school, they always considered him their prize pupil, as well as their pet project! As a result, more frequently than not, he won those coveted school awards such as *"Most Studious,"* and *"Most Likely to Succeed."*

His senior year, Bradley was again in a familiar spot; at the top of his class. He was a striking figure during graduation exercises. Six feet, three inches tall, shoulder length blonde hair and piercing blue eyes. It was obvious to everyone that he had inherited his mother's good looks.

As valedictorian, he made a rousing, motivational speech that impressed everyone from the principal on down.

Because of his high academic achievements, and because of the tireless efforts of several teachers, Bradley became the first student in the history of Cartersville High School to be awarded an academic scholarship to college.

Belinda Sue and Grandma Nell were bewildered. They just shook their heads in amazement, and wondered how all of this could have happened.

It definitely wasn't because of their great success in the area of child rearing. Belinda Sue and Grandma Nell's efforts in child rearing mostly consisted of covering up for Bradley's arrogance, or cleaning up after one of his mischievous schemes.

Belinda Sue had long since worn out her welcome down at Low Boy's. Now 37 years old, she had put on a little weight. Consequently, younger, slimmer girls had taken over her turf.

Her life had been reduced to welfare, food stamps, Saturday night country and western dances, and an occasional one night stand with some old flame.

She and Grandma Nell mostly wasted their days by faithfully watching soap box operas, puffing away on endless cigarettes and gossiping with the girls down at the local beauty parlor.

Of course, Bradley jumped at this opportunity to get out of Cartersville. Again, he really wasn't interested in pursuing academic excellence, and maybe someday becoming a doctor or a lawyer. No, he was just anxious to be delivered from this dried up little town.

He hated the small-mindedness of the town's people, most of whom he considered stupid and fools. He was looking forward to a new environment with exciting new possibilities.

For sure, Bradley had become a good actor. He was very capable of changing his outward demeanor, putting on a good face, and blending into the circumstances when it was to his benefit.

So, it was seemingly a great step forward for the little town of Cartersville when Mayor Raeford Smiley and all the town's folks gave Bradley a great send-off to the big city of San Francisco.

Inwardly though, Bradley's heart had not changed. His attitudes continued to reflect rebellion, insolence and disdain for others; even toward the members of his own family.

Chapter Four

Bradley was greeted by one of those chilly San Francisco mornings as he trudged along with seemingly thousands of other students on the huge campus of Northern California University. This being the first day of classes, he was making his way, hopefully, to Freshman English 101.

After finding the classroom building, which seemed like a mile from his dorm, he found the closest seat possible in the tiered, half-moon shaped classroom.

He looked around, observing the other students. Most were scurrying about like frantic little mice, looking for the best available seats.

Suddenly, Bradley felt a little lonely. *"There must be at least 150 students in this class,"* he thought to himself as he attempted a quick head count. This was not like the small classes at Cartersville High where he was almost always the center of attention. *"I'll bet the professors here don't even bother to learn the names of their students,"* his thoughts continued. *"They probably just teach to a sea of faces and then disappear into the safety of their offices!"*

The gray haired, frumpy dressed, bow tie clad professor barked out the roll call, methodically working his way through the alphabetical listing, never raising his eyes to look at the students.

"Bradley Hawkins," he called.

"Excuse me Sir," Bradley called out, his hand waving high in the air. *"That's Brad. Brad Hawkins!"*

The old, English professor momentarily hesitated and raised an irritated look over a lowered set of reading glasses, making eye contact with Brad. *"Very well,"* he replied somewhat sarcastically, *"Brad Hawkins it is!"*

It wasn't long until Brad was again in a familiar spot, at the head of the class. And, he wasn't just obnoxiously interrupting the classes, trying to impress everyone. He was clearly out performing the other students. Soon, all the professors knew him by name. *"This one has potential,"* they would say!

Toward the end of his second semester, however, Brad was getting bored with the academic environment. He started looking around for some other type of action.

It wasn't long until he found that so-called action; in the form of illegal drugs! Not that he was personally using drugs. He wasn't that stupid! Rather, he became involved in the sales and distribution end of the business.

That summer, Brad didn't bother to go home. He lied to his mom that he had found a summer job, and it was essential that he remain in California.

The truth was, he was making too much money selling drugs on the playgrounds of San Francisco and Oakland.

Belinda Sue and Grandma Nell were, to say the least, greatly disappointed! All year long, they had anxiously looked forward to Bradley's homecoming.

Already, he had skipped the Christmas vacation; opting instead to spend the holidays with his new girlfriend, whom he had met due to head to head competition in Freshman Math.

And now, much to their hurt, he wasn't coming home for the summer either. These days, Bradley's homecoming was just about the only thing they had to look forward to!

As for Brad, he couldn't have cared less about his family. He was enjoying the fruits of his illegal gain.

Already, he had been able to purchase a sporty, little, compact car; and he and his girlfriend were buzzing all over the bay area. He had it made. A full scholarship, a new car, money in his pocket, and a girl to sleep with. He might not ever go back to Cartersville!

"Therefore let him who thinks he stands, take heed lest he fall."

> The Apostle Paul
> First Epistle to the Corinthians
> Chapter 10, verse 12

Chapter Five

Brad's immediate contact and source of supply in the drug trafficking business was a brash, braggart sort of a fellow named Mac Venable.

Mac was one of those guys with a huge ego problem. It was real important for him to be seen wearing designer clothes, gold chains around his neck, rings on almost every finger, and some naive, overdressed, or overexposed young girl on his arm.

He would cruise around town in his steel blue, Porsche convertible; showing up at all the *"trendy"* spots, and flashing around big sums of money.

Brad, on the other hand, was extremely secretive about the drug business; to the extent that not even his roommate had any knowledge of the matter.

He never sold drugs to people he knew; and his distribution points were in sections of San Francisco and Oakland where no one knew him, not even his first name.

He was careful not to draw attention to himself. Sometimes, he would even wear disguises to and from his distribution points.

Beyond Mac, Brad knew no one. He had no idea from who, or from where his supply was coming; and he liked it that way. The less he knew, the better.

Neither was he concerned about the potential destruction of young people's lives. He was only interested in the illegal gain he was enjoying.

As school resumed in the fall, Brad's grades began to drop significantly. He was too busy with his clandestine drug business.

He had also become increasingly bored with the academic environment. In his opinion, the college professors were all a bunch of losers, mired up to their brains in a world of unrealistic theory.

His academic advisors were obviously concerned with this abrupt change. Consequently, he had to endure several seemingly endless counseling sessions.

In some of the counseling sessions, he was challenged to live up to his potential. In others, he was sternly warned about the potential loss of his scholarship.

He responded by doing just the bare minimum to maintain his scholarship.

About halfway through the semester, Brad was watching television one evening in the student lounge of his dorm.

There was news on the TV that night of a big drug bust. More than 30 people had been arrested. Hundreds of pounds of illegal drugs, and hundreds of thousands of dollars had been seized. The newscaster revealed that the drug bust was the culmination of more than nine months of investigation.

Brad began to feel uneasy inside. He wondered if any of those arrested were in his supply line?

He wouldn't have to wait long to find out!

Chapter Six

After classes the next afternoon, Brad was on his way to be resupplied and to turn over the profits of several days sales to Mac Venable.

He followed his standard procedure of mixing up his route and going a slightly different way. Eventually, he would end up at their prearranged rendezvous point, but by changing his route, he wouldn't leave any specific patterns which might be picked up by law enforcement officials.

As he drew near to the rendezvous point, he again had that uneasy feeling in the pit of his stomach.

He was startled when he saw a large area cordoned off with police vehicles, and marked with that yellow tape police use to seal off an area. There were at least 25 police officers blocking the area from hundreds of curious bystanders who were stretching their necks to see what happened.

"*So, what's going on,*" Brad asked one of the bystanders, while at the same time, trying to act casual?

"*Don't know,*" was the reply? "*Some kind of a shoot out, I think.*"

Brad inched closer, peering between people and stretching his six foot, three inch frame to see over the shorter ones.

He finally got close enough to recognize Mac's steel blue, Porsche convertible. It was riddled with bullet holes.

As the crowd began to disperse, he was shaken by what he saw next. There lying on the pavement was a body covered with a white sheet. The sheet, from top to bottom, was deeply stained with blood. Brad later learned that Mac had chosen to shoot it out with police rather than be arrested.

His mind was suddenly joggled back to reality. As he was standing there in plain view of all those police officers, he was reminded that in the little sports bag at his side, there was cocaine, marijuana, a large sum of money, financial records, and a *"hot"* 38 caliber pistol he had obtained from Mac.

He quickly exited the area!

Brad spent the remainder of the day wandering around the Fisherman's Wharf area, trying to clear his head.

Beyond Mac Venable, he had chosen to know no one in the supply line; but did they know him? Had his activities been uncovered in the recent investigation? It was a time of great anxiety!

At the end of the day, Brad made his way back to the Northern Cal campus. He had come to a decision. He knew what he must do.

Later that night, he quietly exited his room, being careful not to wake his roommate.

He slipped by campus security on his way to one of the student parking lots.

He loaded his small, compact car with everything which could tie him to the drug business. The sports bag which contained various amounts of cocaine and marijuana; the cash which he had intended to turn over to Mac; a small black book that contained his financial records; and the 38 caliber pistol. He filled the remainder of the bag with heavy rocks.

He drove for several hours, traveling north up the rocky coastline. There wasn't much traffic on the road that night, so he drove slowly, looking for just the right spot.

Around 3:30 in the morning, he pulled onto the shoulder of the road and got out of the car.

He walked back and forth across the rocky terrain, carefully inspecting the rugged cliffs and the roaring Pacific Ocean below. Half an hour later, he was satisfied that he had found the right spot.

He carefully made his way out to the edge of the cliff. With a mighty heave, he threw the sports bag out over the cliff. He watched, as best he could in the darkness, and listened as the bag splashed into the ocean below, never to be seen again!

Early that same morning, he was waiting on the lot of one of those car dealers that advertise: WE BUY CARS!

He was taking no chances. He was eliminating everything that could possibly link him to the drug business.

Chapter Seven

For the next month, Brad seemed to be a changed person. His attendance in class improved, his grades improved, even his attitude seemed to improve. He demonstrated every appearance of a well adjusted, socially acceptable, young man on the road to a successful life.

But this apparent turnaround was mostly motivated by fear. Fear regarding the possibility that he still might be recognized and arrested for drug trafficking.

After about a month though, the fear subsided. The news coverage became less and less until it was no longer mentioned.

Perhaps he wasn't going to be arrested after all. Maybe the law enforcement agencies didn't know about his involvement. He began to relax.

But, he also began to grow restless once again. It was hard to exist in an environment where he was required to be in some state of submission. He wanted to be in control! He began to look around, trying to find a safer place where he could exert his influence.

One day, while browsing through the Student Activity Center, Brad noticed all kinds of flyers on the bulletin board announcing meetings of various religious groups.

There were flyers encouraging students to attend meetings representing the Black Muslims, Hare Krishna, various sects of the New Age Movement, and also, quite a few Christian groups.

To this point in his life, Brad had never been to church. The closest he had been to any religious gathering was a funeral.

Neither had he ever been interested in, or concerned about anything religious. But, these flyers intrigued him. Something compelled him to check into this matter further.

It didn't take Brad very long to rule out the Hare Krishna, New Age and Eastern Philosophy groups. These people seemed to be lost somewhere in space!

28

Besides, he got bored sitting around meditating, and discussing spiritual theories propagated by some old relic who lived in the mountains of India.

But, the Christian groups were another story. The people who attended the groups were excited and enthusiastic. They acted like they actually believed in God!

Brad also liked the idea of group participation. Anyone could speak up and share what was on their heart.

He especially liked the fact that the participants seemed to be loyal and submissive to their group leaders.

And, of course, they had food after the meetings!

He eventually chose a small Bible study group that didn't seem to have any affiliation with a local church. Oh, they claimed to be a satellite group of some church in Arizona; but in actuality, they were doing their own thing.

The other Christian groups, on the contrary, seemed to be solidly locked into either a national organization, or a local church; and they had pastoral supervision as well as college leadership.

The next afternoon found Brad wandering through the little college village adjacent to the university. He was perusing the book stores, looking for a Bible.

He eventually found one he liked. A used, reference Bible with extensive study helps and limited commentary. He particularly liked the various study helps. With these, he could quickly learn enough to enter into the discussions.

For the remainder of the semester, he researched the Bible diligently. When their Thursday evening meetings were held, he knew the lesson better than anyone, including the leader.

But, there was a major problem. Brad wasn't studying the Bible to know God. He wasn't concerned about the commandments of God in order to govern his life. He wasn't interested in God's promises that offered provision for his life. He was studying for the one purpose of using the scriptures for his own personal gain.

There were those times when he came across portions of scripture which spoke of Jesus Christ and his death for the sins of all mankind.

These times were always accompanied by conviction from the Holy Spirit, challenging him to bow his knee to God. But, he quickly dismissed these feelings. He wasn't interested in any type of submission. He wanted to be in control!

Chapter Eight

During the Christmas holidays, Brad finally went home. It was the first time he had returned to Cartersville in the year and a half since leaving for college.

He dreaded coming back to this dull, dried up, little town, but he didn't have much of a choice. The university closed for the holidays; his ex-girlfriend wasn't very impressed with his new, religious lifestyle; and everyone else in the Bible study group went home for the holidays.

However, to Brad's great surprise, the homecoming turned out rather well!

He didn't expect a heroes welcome, but everywhere he went, the town's folks were bragging on him. *"That's our boy Bradley. He's on the dean's list up at Northern Cal, you know!"*

There were free haircuts at the barber shop; and free lunches at the local, town diner, appropriately named *"Mom's Down Home Cooking."*

And, there was the usual gossip at the beauty parlor, *"Well, it's just amazing that Bradley turned out as well as he did. He didn't have the best of backgrounds, you know; what with Belinda Sue prostituting herself down at Low Boy's!"*

The university vacation period started earlier than the Christmas holidays in the Cartersville school system. Consequently, the high school principal asked Brad to speak to the senior class. As usual, he impressed everyone with a humorous, but serious talk about working hard and staying in school.

He was even invited to speak to the entire student body at Cartersville Elementary School about the dangers of drugs.

One day when Brad, Belinda Sue and Grandma Nell were enjoying some free turkey and stuffing at Mom's diner, Mayor Raeford Smiley came over to their table.

"We're all very proud of you, Bradley," he exclaimed. Brad put on a good face, and mustered up an acceptable, *"thank you."*

"Of course," continued Mayor Smiley, *"there was that short period of time when your grades suffered a little lapse; but Dean Helms from up at Northern Cal assured me that you were now back on the right track."*

"Oh, I understand," he continued. *"We all go through those little periods of stress. But, I was pleased to see you bounce back."*

As Mayor Smiley began greeting other people, Brad breathed a seething response through his teeth, *"it never ceases to amaze me, how everyone in this little, rat hole town knows your business."*

Belinda Sue and Grandma Nell weren't upset. They were beaming! In a way, they were sort of like celebrities when Brad was around. It was one of the few things they had to be excited about these days.

At the annual, family Christmas gathering, Grandma Nell went on and on, bragging about Bradley's accomplishments.

Uncle Frank and Aunt Pearl were pretty much disgusted by all this attention on Brad. Their children had not achieved such lofty success. With great restraint, they managed to hold their tongue!

Richard, who was two years older than Brad, had moved up to southern Colorado, and was working as a ranch hand.

Timothy, a year younger than Brad, had dropped out of high school after his junior year. He was pumping gas at one of the two service stations in Cartersville.

And Glenda, who always had a crush on Brad, was clerking at the local five and dime.

As for Brad, he was eating up all this special attention.

Between accolades, however, he managed to show contempt for Uncle Frank and Aunt Pearl.

He also seized upon every opportunity to make Richard and Timothy look ignorant; and reveled in their obvious jealousy.

And Glenda; he gave her just enough attention to keep her clamoring for more.

It was clear in his mind that he was the dominant member of the family, and most likely, the whole town!

Chapter Nine

When Brad returned to Northern Cal after the Christmas holidays, there was a surprise waiting. The leader of their Bible study group had unexpectedly dropped out of school.

As the group met together, there was a lot of discussion, but mostly confusion about what to do. Someone suggested they contact the church in Arizona; but another explained that this so-called affiliation was in word only, and never formerly organized. As the discussion wound down, talk turned toward disbanding the group.

Someone piped up from the back of the room with a final attempt at concluding the matter, *"how about Brad Hawkins? Maybe he would like to take over? Most of the time, he knew the lesson better than our former leader anyway!"*

Suddenly, all eyes were on Brad.

"Well," he acted surprised, *"I suppose I could give it a try."*

And, so began Brad Hawkins' stint as Bible study leader. It was what he wanted all along, to be in control!

Brad began to spend hours going over passages of scripture to find just the right emphasis for his lessons. He sat in his room for long periods of time, meditating about what he would teach, and how he would present the material. He didn't pray! He didn't know how to pray! He didn't know God!

His teachings were cleverly prepared so as not to offend anyone; and certainly not to challenge anyone! The messages were filled with love, forgiveness and acceptance for everyone. There was not even a hint of such things as repentance, faith, commitment or obedience.

Soon, the Bible study began to grow. Brad's message was a popular one; always love and acceptance, regardless of a person's lifestyle! Consequently, the group began to fill up with some *"rare birds."*

There were still a few baby Christians in the group. Those who had little or no foundation of God's word in their lives.

There were others from liberal denominational backgrounds who referred to themselves as Christians, although their lifestyles didn't reflect the principles of the Bible.

Then, there were a few self-proclaimed philosophers who admitted to being Christian as well as a little of everything else. They viewed the Bible as just one of many holy books from which mankind could draw enlightenment.

Brad carefully fed them exactly what they needed to hear in order to superficially sooth their consciences!

He rarely received any challenge to his teaching. One night a young girl, a visitor stood in the midst of the group. *"Excuse me, but all I hear in this group is how God loves us, and how he accepts us just as we are. What about repentance from sin? What about accepting Jesus Christ as Savior, and trusting in his shed blood for forgiveness of sins? Only then are we truly accepted by God!"*

There were a few snickers from the liberal contingent.

One of the so-called enlightened members tried, unsuccessfully, to expound upon a wild theory about the evolution of God's thoughts.

Lastly, several young men of a homosexual persuasion had heard all they could take, and angrily told the visitor to sit down.

And Brad, he once again momentarily experienced conviction from the Holy Spirit; but he quickly rejected it.

Instead, he cunningly responded to the challenge with cleverly placed, seemingly logical words of explanation, which satisfied the group, and shamed the visitor.

"Some indeed preach Christ even from envy and strife, and some also from good will: THE FORMER PREACH CHRIST FROM SELFISH AMBITION, NOT SINCERELY...."

> The Apostle Paul
> Epistle to the Philippians
> Chapter 1, verses 15-16

Chapter Ten

Summer break was a big bore. After about a week of accolades from the Cartersville Town's folks, Brad became weary of their small town mentality.

He became especially weary of Belinda Sue and Grandma Nell's uneventful, daily routine.

He was restless to get back to school, and to his so-called Bible study group. The little group, which was about 12 in number when he took over the leadership, had grown to more than 50 prior to the summer break.

One day, while enjoying the extended hospitality and generosity at Mom's diner,

Mayor Raeford Smiley came over and sat down at their table.

"You know, Bradley," he began, *"I've been meaning to have a talk with you. I'm glad we finally have this opportunity. After you graduate from Northern Cal, I'd like for you to think about coming back here to Cartersville. As you know, Mr. James, our town manager is getting on in years. I expect he'll be about ready to retire in a couple of years. You might be just the man for that spot."*

Brad almost laughed in his face. The very thought of moving back to Cartersville almost made him want to throw up. Instead, he responded in his usual controlled and calculated manner, *"that's very encouraging to hear, Mayor Smiley. I'm honored that you would consider me for such a position. I definitely will keep it in mind."*

After a month and a half of sweltering around in the Cartersville heat, Brad couldn't take any more of this little, dead-end town.

He hitched a ride to a nearby town, and purchased a brand new Harley-Davidson motorcycle with some of the money he had stashed away from his former drug business.

Amidst disappointment and complaints from Belinda Sue and Grandma Nell, Brad packed his things and hit the road; heading southeast toward Waco, Texas.

One of the members of his study group at Northern Cal had shared some interesting stories with him about a religious commune of people near Waco.

If he remembered correctly, they called themselves something like Branch Davidian; and their leader was a young man who went by the name of David Koresh.

It didn't take Brad very long to receive directions to their compound. It seems that they were already somewhat of a legend in the area.

For the next six weeks, Brad became a member of the group. He was impressed, in fact, somewhat mesmerized by the teachings of this man, David Koresh.

This was his first exposure to teaching on the subject of the end times; and although he wasn't too sure about the validity of the teaching, he nonetheless took copious notes, and made a promise to himself to look deeper into the matter at a later date.

Brad was especially impressed by the group's strong work ethic; and he was even more impressed with the loyalty and submission of the group's members toward David Koresh.

At the same time, he was somewhat disturbed by what seemed to be a militant attitude within the group. He heard a rumor that the group was arming themselves for a possible confrontation with law enforcement officials.

Overall, however, he considered this experience as very valuable. He pondered in his mind whether it would be possible to implement some of these new ideas in his own group back at Northern Cal.

Toward the end of the summer vacation, he packed up his few belongings, and began the long motorcycle trek back to the San Francisco bay area.

Chapter Eleven

As Brad's junior year at Northern Cal began, so did the Bible study. He tracked down everyone who had attended during the Spring Semester. Soon, they were buzzing again with activity.
But, Brad wasn't content with the size of the group. He had his sights set on bigger things. He had colorful, professional looking flyers printed, and posted them all over campus.
And, there was one very significant change. The group was no longer referred to as a Bible study. Brad renamed it, *"The Spiritual Workshop."*

Some of the teachings were still from the Bible. Carefully selected portions of scripture, frequently twisted, taken out of context, and then applied in a way that was advantageous to Brad's objectives.

But, the teachings were now intermixed with quotes and ideas from other so-called holy men. In particular, Brad quoted some of the teachings of his new spiritual hero, David Koresh.

His six weeks at the Branch Davidian compound had left an impression upon him; as if another spirit was influencing him.

Yet, the cornerstone of his doctrine continued to be the strong emphasis on high self-esteem.

As for the members of the group, they couldn't discern any major changes. Just another slant on the subject of the end times.

The few born again Christians that remained in the group were themselves being deceived. Because of the fact that scriptures were used during the teaching sessions, and because the words of Jesus were sometimes quoted, they were convinced that the group must be all right. Their lack of a strong biblical foundation prevented them from discerning between good and evil.

There was no longer any question or confusion about who was in charge. Brad was solidly entrenched as the group's leader; to the extent that they began to take on a new identity.

It would now be difficult to find anyone in the group who was a disciple of Jesus Christ. They were all very evidently becoming disciples of Brad Hawkins!

Brad let his hair grow long, and braided it into blonde dreadlocks like those of the Rastafarian movement. He grew a scruffy beard, and wore faded jeans, sandals, and white corduroy parkas, which gave him the look of some sort of guru.

All of his efforts paid off. Attendance at *"The Spiritual Workshop"* increased to around 75 each Thursday night.

Brad Hawkins was quickly becoming the most visible, spiritual presence on campus. Everywhere he went, members of *"The Spiritual Workshop"* tagged along like little groupies.

At the Student Activity Center, he engaged in fruitless debates with members of campus Christian organizations like: Intervarsity Christian Fellowship, and Campus Crusade For Christ, on such subjects as the validity and relativity of the Bible in today's modern society.

In the *"Great Religions of the World"* class, he took more than his share of time to expound upon the different religious schools of thought.

In reality, Brad knew extremely little about true spiritual matters. His words and actions would remind us of a description written by Jude, the brother of Jesus,

"....they mouth great swelling words, flattering people to gain advantage."

Yet, Brad continued to pursue this path of spiritual pride and arrogance. It was as if these words of scripture were literally being fulfilled, *"Professing to be wise, they became fools."*

"Every word of God is pure....do not add to His words, lest He reprove you, and you be found a liar."

                The sayings of Agur
                The book of Proverbs
                From Chapter 30, verses 5-6

Chapter Twelve

During the course of Brad's junior year at Northern Cal, four significant things took place that proved to be decisive in shaping the direction of his future.

He continued to make good grades in order to maintain his scholarship; but make no mistake about it, his primary emphasis during this time was on developing the *"The Spiritual Workshop."*

The first significant thing was that people other than university students began to attend *"The Spiritual Workshop."*

At first, it was a few former students who were still hanging around the college community. In time, however, other people began to attend, including couples with children and even a few senior citizens.

Most were people who had been hurt, rejected, or in some way, stressed out with life, and were now searching for acceptance and love.

This broadened Brad's thinking. He began to see himself in a different light. Someone who appealed to all social and economic groups.

The second significant happening, and the ultimate results it would produce, speaks for itself.

One of the senior citizens, an elderly lady who was attending the group, came up to Brad after one of the meetings. She voiced her praise, *"Son, I want you to know how much these spiritual workshops have helped me. You are such a compassionate and caring young man. Before I started attending these workshops, I had such a problem with low self-esteem, but I seem to be getting better every time I hear you teach. God bless you!"*

Then, she quietly and privately placed three, crisp, new, one hundred dollar bills into his shirt pocket.

Thirdly, attendance at the workshops exceeded 100, causing university officials to voice their concerns about the logistics of the group.

"The Spiritual Workshop" was using a large meeting room in the Student Activity Center. The staff there had expressed concern about the disarray of the room after meetings.

A more serious and underlying concern was the increase in the number of outsiders attending the meetings, especially those who were formerly registered students.

Brad solved this problem by renting a large room over a local restaurant about one block off campus. A quick passing of the hat easily provided enough money for the modest rent.

This opened the door for even more outsiders to attend. So much so, that people no longer viewed *"The Spiritual Workshop"* as a university activity. Instead, they began to view the workshop as a community outreach!

Fourthly, in the Spring of that year, Brad received word from Cartersville that Grandma Nell had passed away.

It was a completely unexpected heart attack that suddenly snatched away her life without so much as the courtesy of a warning.

Belinda Sue was an emotional wreck, but Brad ignored her pleas to come home for the funeral. If Grandma Nell was dead, she was dead! There was nothing he could do to change the situation.

This pretty much severed his ties with Cartersville. The only person he was ever close to was Grandma Nell. He never had much of a relationship with his mom, or his other relatives, and he didn't intend to start now!

In the ensuing months, Brad devoted himself more and more to *"The Spiritual Workshop."* It was as if this was now his family, and these were now his people!

His actual relatives had always looked down on him. They had never shown him any respect or appreciation. They always considered him the *"black sheep"* of the family.

Well, he would show them. His success would soon surpass anything his stupid relatives had ever accomplished. He would show them. He would show them all!

Chapter Thirteen

As the Spring semester ended, Brad made a monumental decision. He changed the meeting time from Thursday evening to Sunday morning.

"The Spiritual Workshop" was now essentially a church. Brad incorporated the group under the name: *"Church of the Open Heart,"* and subsequently appointed himself as pastor.

All kinds of people from all over the bay area began to attend the church, as if they were being drawn by a magnet. Whatever their lot in life, they were accepted and loved.

There was never any requirement to change one's lifestyle. *"God loves you, and we love you, just as you are,"* continued to be Pastor Brad's central theme.

The attitudes and actions of the people were reflected in their loose lifestyles. Their walk, their talk, and their dress ranged from sensual to professional. From an outsiders viewpoint, they were a motley bunch.

But, there was also a deceptive binding together among the people. The emphasis on loving and accepting one another caused this bonding among a group of people who otherwise had little, or no direction for their lives.

And, there was just enough of a spiritual glaze over the situation to keep things respectable.

That summer the church increased to more than 200. The services were exciting and enthusiastic.

A talented array of young musicians, some from Northern Cal's School of Music, created their own unique style and sound of music on guitars, keyboards, flutes, violins, bongo drums and even a dulcimer.

Carefully selected songs, which fit in with the church's philosophy, were vigorously sang.

Emotional testimonies were shared, all of which glorified Pastor Brad Hawkins, and explained how his teaching and ministry had helped people.

Then, there was Brad's message. He had become a very accomplished speaker, blending soft, easy to hear teaching with inspirational, authoritative preaching.

To sum up this whole matter, one might say that Brad Hawkins had progressed from his little game of trying to impress everyone as a campus Bible study leader. He was now on a full-fledged power trip.

In the Fall, Brad didn't register for his senior year at Northern Cal. He couldn't have cared less about school. He had found his calling in life.

Attendance in the church continued to increase and topped 300 around the end of October.

A liberal, local newspaper did a full page article on the church for their religion section. This boosted the church to 400 during the Christmas holidays.

Local pastors began to warn their congregations from their pulpits, and via radio and television broadcasts about the deceptiveness of the church.

Brad took advantage of these attacks, as he called them, by likening himself and the church to the persecution that Jesus and the early church received.

Unfortunately, there were still a small number of born again Christians who continued to attend the church.

It's true that some of them were there because they lacked a strong foundation of God's word in their lives; and thus, they were unable to discern between truth and deception.

But, sadly, there were other Christians who had recently joined the church.

These were rebellious Christians who were unwilling to submit to genuine spiritual authority. *"The Church of the Open Heart"* offered them the conscience soothing convenience of being involved in a church, while at the same time, allowing them to do their own thing.

"But there were also false prophets among the people, even as there will be false teachers among you....BEGUILING UNSTABLE SOULS"

> Second Epistle of the Apostle Peter
> From Chapter 2, verses 1, 14

Chapter Fourteen

Ferguson Whitney was a godly man. He had walked with God, serving him fulltime for more than 53 years. Now 75 years old, he was still strong and robust, not just spiritually, but also physically and mentally.

Over the years, the anointing and power of God manifested through his life had increased until he now legitimately ministered in the office of the prophet.

Brother Whitney had traveled all over the world, teaching the word of God and prophetically speaking the mind of Christ into the lives of believers, including other ministers and pastors.

He was now recognized and deeply respected as a genuine prophet of God throughout the body of Christ both nationally and internationally.

As Brother Whitney was teaching at a Greater Bay Area Minister's Conference, some of the pastors in attendance began to share concerns about this upstart *"Church of the Open Heart."*

They weren't just concerned about the deception in the church. There had been almost every type of deception imaginable throughout the bay area for decades.

What troubled these local pastors was the fact that young, immature, born again Christians were being deceived. Several of these pastors had actually lost members to Brad Hawkins' church.

This grieved Brother Whitney's heart. For sure, he had a burden for lost people who were caught up in the various cults. He longed to see them come to the knowledge of the truth, accept Jesus Christ as Savior and Lord, and be delivered from the bondage of deception.

But, this matter was entirely different. Here were born again children of God who were being deceived. Some of them had left strong, Bible believing churches, and were now involved in *"The Church of the Open Heart."*

Brad's primary doctrine of loving and accepting everyone was a real drawing card.

To these young Christians, who often struggled with their flesh, *"The Church of the Open Heart"* offered the option of continuing a sinful lifestyle, while being assured that God loves you and accepts you just like you are!

One cold, wintry morning, about one month after teaching and ministering for the Greater Bay Area Minister's Conference, Ferguson Whitney was stoking the fire and placing a new log into his huge, brick fireplace.

All morning, he had been troubled in his spirit. For several hours, he had paced throughout his home in southern Oregon, praying and waiting upon the Lord.

Suddenly, the Spirit of the Lord spoke clearly and precisely into his spirit, *"My son, I want you to return to the bay area, go to The Church of the Open Heart, and deliver a strong warning to Brad Hawkins regarding the deception he is propagating among my people."*

This didn't come as a great surprise to Brother Whitney. As a prophet of the Lord, he had been called upon before to deliver warnings to other false teachers and false prophets.

Without hesitation, be began to pack an overnight bag and make arrangements to return to San Francisco.

On the short commuter flight down to San Francisco, he began to think about the task before him. A little compassion welled up in his heart. From what he had been told, Brad Hawkins was very young. *"Perhaps it's not too late to turn him around,"* he thought? *"Someone as gifted as this young man could be a real asset to the kingdom of God."*

Yet, he would have to be firm. His primary mission was to deliver a warning. He recalled the conversation between Jesus and his disciples in the 24th. chapter of the gospel of Matthew.

"....what will be the sign of Your coming, and of the end of the age? And Jesus answered and said to them: take heed that no one deceives you....many false prophets will rise up and deceive many."

Chapter Fifteen

It had not been a good day for Brad. With almost 500 people in attendance, the church was *"bursting at the seams,"* literally overflowing the large room they had rented above the restaurant.

All day long he had been on the phone looking for a bigger place to meet, but so far, with no success.

His day had already been interrupted twice by annoying phone calls that wasted his time.

First, it was Dean Helms, his former academic advisor from Northern Cal.

"Brad, I've been on the phone with your mother. We both want to encourage you to return to school. I'm certain I can have your scholarship reinstated."

Next, there was Belinda Sue, begging and pleading with him to return to school; and then begging and pleading with him to come home for a visit.

To put it bluntly, he was *"steamed!"* His mom, who had accomplished zero with her life, surely didn't have any right to try to direct his life!

Besides, it greatly irritated him that nobody apart from his congregation was taking his church seriously. He was a source of enlightenment in a dark world, and nobody seemed to care!

Then came the third interruption. The church secretary, Naomi Peterson apologetically slipped into the office, quietly closing the door behind her.

Naomi Peterson was a pretty, young, African-American girl with deep spiritual roots over several generations. Unfortunately, those spiritual roots were based mostly upon religious tradition rather than the word of God!

She had been drawn to Brad because he seemed to be going somewhere! The one thing Naomi did not want in life was to be a nobody, going nowhere!

In whispered tones, she explained her intrusion, *"I know you told me not to disturb you, but there's this old man outside who absolutely will not go away! I told him you were not seeing anyone today, but he says he will wait in the reception area, no matter how long it takes, until you will see him."*

"What," Brad exploded. *"Exactly who is this old man; some street person?"*

"I don't think so," explained Naomi. *"He's sort of distinguished looking. He says he has a message from God!"*

Brad had always liked a challenge. He considered himself superior to almost everyone, and equal to any challenge that came his way.

With a look of scorn and determination on his face, he threw his pencil on the desk, and said, *"all right then, show the old boy in!"*

Ferguson Whitney wasted no time with hand shakes, introductions or niceties.

"Young man," he boldly spoke forth, *"I am a prophet of the Lord God Almighty. About this time yesterday, the Spirit of God spoke to me and instructed me to warn you about the deception in your own heart, and the deception you are propagating among the people in your church.*

You have failed to teach them truth. You have not commanded them to repent. Neither have you given them the remedy for sin.

You have failed to do so because you are not building God's kingdom. You are attempting to establish and build your own kingdom.

Furthermore, the Lord would say unto you: unless you repent, and lead the people into the way of truth, your efforts will surely not succeed. Your kingdom will be utterly torn down, and the remembrance of it will disappear from the earth!"

Initially, Brad was stunned. It felt like the blood had literally drained out of his face. He had never encountered anyone like this old man.

And, once again, for a brief moment, there was that feeling he didn't like; the conviction of the Holy Spirit.

More than once he had convinced himself that he was genuinely helping people; but, somewhere deep in his heart, there was this nagging feeling that he was just a big fake.

However, after struggling with his conscience for a few moments, his pride once again reasserted itself upon the throne of his life.

Now, he was experiencing a new feeling; anger!

Almost in a rage, he leaped from his seat. *"Just who do you think you are? You self-righteous old fool! Who gives you the right to judge me? You get the Hell out of my office!"*

The burden that was upon Ferguson Whitney for the past 24 hours had lifted. As he departed the office, he had peace in his heart, knowing that he had obeyed the Lord; but there was also sadness for those under Brad Hawkins' persuasion.

As he stepped into the waiting taxi, he recalled a scripture from Romans 1:28, *"And even as they did not like to retain God in their knowledge, God gave them over to a debased mind, to do those things which are not fitting."*

"....Believe in the Lord your God, and you shall be established; believe His prophets, and you shall prosper."

Second Book of the Chronicles
From Chapter 20, verse 20

Chapter Sixteen

During the Spring of what should have been Brad's senior year at Northern California University, three monumental events occurred; all of which proved to be instrumental in shaping the remainder of his life.

The first major event began to unfold in February at the Branch Davidian compound in Waco, Texas.

Brad's spiritual hero, David Koresh had gotten into trouble with federal law enforcement agencies. He and his followers had killed several federal agents, which resulted in a month and a half standoff.

Ultimately, David Koresh and those who remained with him perished in a great fire that engulfed their compound during an assault by law enforcement officers.

Brad was shaken and angered by this horrible event. He had frequently quoted David Koresh. For several Sundays thereafter, he preached long and hard about the loss of religious freedom and the lack of justice in America. His congregation of around 500 echoed their agreement.

Despite this outward display of strength and indignation; inwardly he was suffering from depression because of this ordeal. He was seriously considering quitting, but then, he would lose everything he had built.

By this time, the Christian community viewed Brad as a dangerously deceptive person, and a likely candidate as the next major cult leader.

Yet, in his own eyes, and in the eyes of his congregation, he was a very successful and sensitive pastor, offering an alternative from the narrow-mindedness of fundamental Christianity.

But right now, he was confused. He did not want to follow the path of failure that David Koresh had trod. He desperately needed guidance about the future.

Of course, he would never admit to any other person that he needed guidance; and humbling himself before God, if there was a God, was not an option.

The second major event began around the end of April, while Brad was still trying to recover from the David Koresh disaster. After more than two years of legal battles, those who had been arrested in the big drug bust were finally being brought to trial.

Every day for more than a month, Brad nervously watched the local news with fear and anxiety.

Mac Venable's name became a household word. His gun battle with San Francisco police was the central focus of the trial. It seems that Mac was higher up the ladder of authority than Brad had realized.

He was afraid that his name still might surface during the trial. Evidence was being heard from undercover agents, informers, and those who had been granted immunity in exchange for their testimony.

Again, he was seriously considering quitting. This time however, he was not just considering quitting, but fleeing the country as well. The church had built up a rather large cash reserve. He could withdraw the money and simply disappear.

He paced the floor at nights, worrying about an uncertain future. More than ever, he desperately needed some sort of guidance or direction.

His Bible lay on the living room floor. The wisdom of God was as close as an arm's reach; but he was too proud to admit that he needed divine guidance.

He had always been self-sufficient and in control, and somehow, he would work out these problems also.

The last monumental event was yet to come, but it was the one that would eliminate all the concerns created by the first two events.

It would literally shape the future for the remainder of Brad Hawkins' life!

Book Two

The Visitation

"Test all things; hold fast to what is good."

> The Apostle Paul
> First Epistle to the Thessalonians
> Chapter 5, verse 21

Chapter Seventeen

It was 3:00 in the morning, but Brad couldn't sleep for worrying. He was restless, pacing back and forth throughout his little apartment. He was becoming paranoid over these problems.

Naomi Peterson, the church secretary, and Brad's part-time *"live-in"* girlfriend was aroused from her sleep. *"What's the matter with you Brad? You've been pacing around the floor all night like some caged leopard. Come to bed and get some sleep!"*

"Sorry," Brad replied, *"I didn't mean to wake you. I'll go into the living room."* He closed the bedroom door behind him.

He had been through several months of torment in his mind. The anger over the David Koresh situation; the anxiety about the drug bust trial; and also, to be honest, the words of that old man, Ferguson Whitney were still haunting him.

As morning slowly approached, Brad continued to pace back and forth. Should he continue, or should he quit? *"I must make a decision on this matter soon,"* he thought.

Suddenly, he was surprised, and somewhat startled by the appearance of a small, but very bright light in the darkest corner of his living room.

He wondered about the source of the light, realizing it was still a bit early for the initial rays of the sun to penetrate his little apartment.

He watched intently as the light slowly expanded in circumference until it saturated the entire corner of the room.

"What on earth is this," he wondered, his pulse rate quickening? The puzzled look on his face grew more intense?

He was visibly shaken as the glowing figure of a man materialized in the light. He was dressed in what appeared to be ancient, Persian battle array. Brad felt like the hair on his body was standing straight up!

He involuntarily sank to his knees as this image of a man opened his eyes, revealing the mystical semblance of trying to see into a dark, endless cavern.

The image pointed a finger, seemingly into Brad's eyes, and spoke in a low but powerful voice, *"I have come from heavenly places. I am the angel, Micah-Ahmid, come to deliver a message from God!"*

"What does God want," Brad struggled to get the words out through a weak, quivering voice?

"You are one of God's chosen ones," continued the angel. *"You are one of his messiahs."*

Brad never had much of an interest or belief in the supernatural, but now, he was all ears!

The angel continued to deliver the message, *"Many messiahs whom God has chosen have failed. Your friend, David Koresh failed because he chose the way of violence. Jesus Christ failed because he offended the political and religious leaders of his day. Many others have also failed, but now God has chosen you as a messiah to the people."*

"And, what does God require of me?" Brad was slowly regaining his composure.

"This day, God is commanding you to deliver your people from the corruption, pollution, violence and injustice of this land, and move to a new, promised land which he will show you."

This part suited Brad just fine. He was not only willing, but ready to get as far away as possible from the current problems and anxieties he was facing.

The angel continued the message, *"God has, this day, given you a new name. No longer will you be called by the name, Brad Hawkins. From this day forward, you shall be called by your new, spiritual, messianic name, which is: Christopher Judah!"*

With that, the angel's image seemed to dissolve into the light. The circle of light then slowly decreased in circumference and brightness until it disappeared into the darkness of the early morning.

Brad sat perfectly still, and quiet for a long time. He could hear the beating of his heart. Over and over again, he meditated on the visitation. There was no doubt that the visitation was genuine. He wasn't the type to imagine such things.

Around 6:30 in the morning, just as the rays of the sun began to peek into the little apartment, he made his decision.

Standing to his feet, he gazed for a few moments into the now lifeless corner, and then declared, *"I will obey the instructions of the angel!"*

---

*"*And no wonder! For Satan himself transforms himself into an angel of light. Therefore it is no great thing if his ministers also transform themselves into ministers of righteousness....*"*

The Apostle Paul
Second Epistle to the Corinthians
Chapter 11, verses 14-15

Chapter Eighteen

The next day found Brad at the public library researching the meaning and significance of his new name.

He discovered that one meaning of the name, *"Christopher,"* is: *"Bearer of Christ."*

Remembering the angel's message, he reasoned that this must mean he had been chosen by God to be a messiah to the people in the same manner that Jesus Christ had previously been chosen.

Next, he discovered that the name, *"Judah"* referred to one of the sons of the Old Testament Patriarch, Jacob.

Later, the name referred to an ancient tribe of Israel, named after Judah, the son of Jacob.

The name literally meant, *"Celebrated,"* or *"Praise."*

He paused from his research for a few minutes to think about this new last name, *"Judah!"*

He fantasized about great celebrations in his honor. Was he destined to receive the admiration and praise that other messiahs had received?

He then remembered that the angel said other messiahs had failed! Well, he would be more careful than the others. He didn't intend to fail!

Next, he discovered that *"Messiah"* is defined as, *"anointed."* This seemed to refer to someone who was equipped, or empowered to be a deliverer.

"Evidently," Brad reasoned, *"I must already be anointed because of my natural ability to lead people and take control of situations."*

He discovered that the word, *"Messiah"* could also refer to someone who, *"professed to be, or was accepted as the leader of some hope or cause."*

He could easily envision himself in this role, but he might need help in convincing the people. He hoped the angel, Micah-Ahmid might reappear and supernaturally provide that help?

As he continued to meditate about the visitation, he recalled another key part of the angel's message. God was instructing him to move to a new place; to lead the people to a promised land that he would give them.

"Promised land," he thought to himself. *"God is going to give us our own promised land, and I'll be in control of it!"*

He found the place in the book of the Exodus, and read and re-read the account of Moses delivering the Children of Israel out of the bondage of Egypt to their promised land.

He thought for a while on the things he had discovered. He concluded that as God's chosen messiah, he was to go forth in the same manner or likeness as Jesus Christ, but succeeding where the angel said Jesus Christ and other messiahs had failed.

He was to lead his people to their own promised land where they would live a life of peace and prosperity. There, they would experience freedom from the bondage of corruption, pollution, violence and injustice that was strangling the whole world.

In a manner of speaking, They would create their own heaven here on earth!

He didn't know what would happen to the people after death. Right now, it didn't seem to be all that important. There were too many plans to be made, and too much work to be done to establish that perfect environment right here on the earth!

Brad never considered looking into the scriptures to see if all these things agreed with the word of God.

Anyway, it didn't matter since he didn't accept the Bible as a source of authority for his life. He had made his decision. He believed the visitation! He believed the angel's message!

"But evil men and impostors will grow worse and worse, deceiving AND BEING DECEIVED."

>The Apostle Paul
>Second Epistle to Timothy
>Chapter 3, verse 13

Chapter Nineteen

The next Sunday, there was a noticeable difference in Brad. One elderly lady commented, *"Pastor Brad looks like he's seen an angel!"*

Brad openly and dramatically shared the visitation. Some members of the congregation were skeptical, but everyone was on the edge of their seat.

A whispering swept through the people as he explained that the angel had instructed him to move the church from the corruption, pollution, violence and injustice of the bay area to a new, promised land that God would show them.

"Is this going to be another Jim Jones thing," someone asked, referring to the San Francisco based People's Temple that moved to the South American nation of Guyana, and subsequently ended when all the members died in a tragic suicide?

"Absolutely not," answered Brad, *"but God has revealed to me that I'm to lead you to our own promised land."*

Many of the people were not able to make this kind of commitment. They were established in the bay area. Established in jobs, established in homes, and their children established in schools. Their extended families were here. They just couldn't make such a drastic change. It was inevitable that the church would lose a significant number of people.

Surprisingly though, when the call for commitment was made, around 350 of the 500 or so members stood to their feet.

Most were idealistic young people who were students or former students at Northern California University. But, there were also married couples with no ties; and elderly people with nothing to hold them to the bay area. Lastly, there were quite a few homeless people!

Brad continued to explain the visitation. The angel had given him a new name. No longer was he to be called Brad Hawkins. From this day forth, he was to be called by his new, spiritual name: Christopher Judah!

As he explained the meaning of his new name, some of those who were not able to make the commitment to move, raised their eyebrows, and glanced at one another with questionable looks.

"It appears, Pastor Brad," one of them commented, *"that you are having illusions of grandeur! You seem to be fashioning yourself into some kind of messiah!"*

This irritated Brad. He spoke out with anger in his voice, quoting both Jesus and the Old Testament warrior, Joshua, *"He who is not with me is against me....choose for yourselves this day whom you will serve."*

"Oh come on, Brad," another replied, *"We've known you for almost four years. Aren't you taking this visitation thing a bit too serious?"*

Brad continued with his authoritative and angry outburst. *"Those of you who are not with me, I insist, I demand that you leave this church immediately!"*

This sent a shock wave throughout the church. At first, everyone just sat there, stunned and silent. Then, there was a rustling about, a gathering of personal belongings and a shuffling of feet. A few minutes later, they were all gone!

Then, something mysterious and amazing happened. For more than two hours Brad spoke prophetically into the people's lives; speaking things that were heretofore hidden!

He uncovered the secrets of their past. He revealed things that were currently happening in their lives. He gave them directions for their future.

The people were shocked, but captivated by this psychic happening. Some were crying about the words he had spoken to them. Thoughts were racing through their minds. *"Surely, this man has experienced a genuine, supernatural visitation. Perhaps he really is a messiah!"*

Most of these prophetic words revealed hurts of the past, and wounds that still lingered. The very reasons why most of the people found their way to *"The Church of the Open Heart,"* and to Brad Hawkins in the first place.

One young girl sprang to her feet and emotionally declared, *"Christopher Judah, you are my messiah. I will follow you to this new promised land!"*

"For false christs and false prophets will arise and SHOW GREAT SIGNS AND WONDERS, so as to deceive, if possible, even the elect."

Jesus Christ
The Gospel of Matthew
Chapter 24, verse 24

Chapter Twenty

It was the next Tuesday morning after that strange, but eventful Sunday. Elsie Mae Thompson was waiting in the reception area of the church office.

Momma Elsie, as she was called, was the oldest member of the church, 79 years young.

The church meant a great deal to her. After her husband passed away, she had felt detached from life. Her children, who lived thousands of miles away, paid her little or no attention. They were too busy with their own lives.

In a manner of speaking, the church had become her family. It had rescued her from a life of loneliness. She looked upon Brad Hawkins like he was her own son.

"*Momma Elsie, please come in,*" Brad was peering out of his office. "*What can I do for you this bright, sunshiny morning?*"

"*And a good morning to you, Pastor Brad.*" Momma Elsie struggled just a bit getting to her feet, but for the most part, she was still strong and in good health.

"*Oh, I'm so sorry,*" She hesitated for a moment on her way into Brad's office. "*I should have said Pastor Christopher.*"

"*Just Christopher will do fine,*" said Brad. "*I'm going to stop using the title: pastor. We're all a family, you know.*"

Momma Elsie looked about for the most comfortable chair, and plopped herself down. "*I know you're busy,*" she continued, "*and I don't want to take up too much of your time; but what I came to see you about, well, it's about the land God promised you.*"

Brad's attention suddenly perked up, "*Yes, go on.*"

"*Well, years ago my husband owned a ranch up in the mountains of Colorado. We had cattle, horses, a tractor, ranch hands. Oh, at one time it was a fine ranch!*

Well, when my husband got too old to run the ranch, we moved out here to San Francisco; but you know, he never sold that ranch.

Of course, when he died, he left the ranch to me; but I've never had much of an interest, nor the energy to revive the ranch, especially by myself.

Now, I don't know if you're even interested in this ranch, but I thought I would at least mention it."

"yes, yes, I'm very interested," Brad's heart was pounding with excitement!

"Well Pastor Brad. Oh, sorry again, I meant to say, Christopher! If you think the church could use this ranch, then I'm willing to give it to you."

Christopher's interest and enthusiasm increased as Momma Elsie, in her somewhat slow and overly thorough manner, continued to describe the ranch.

"Momma Elsie," Christopher finally concluded, *"you are such a blessing to this church. Even if the ranch doesn't turn out to be our promised land, your attitude is still an inspiration to all of us."*

Momma Elsie beamed with satisfaction as she left the office. She was being hugged on one side by Christopher, and on the other side by Naomi. It was so very good to be appreciated!

Rushing back to the office, Christopher frantically began making arrangements for a trip to Colorado to *"spy out the land!"* He was on one phone, calling airlines. Naomi was on the other phone, calling hotels and rental car companies.

"*This is so exciting,*" exclaimed Naomi during a short pause between phone calls!

Christopher ignored her, and continued making arrangements.

"*Take me with you,*" she pleaded!

"*No,*" Christopher gave her a disgusted look. "*Stay here and do the job you were hired to do!*"

"*Yeah, I understand,*" chided Naomi as she stormed out, slamming the office door behind her. "*I'm good enough to share your bed, but not good enough to help run your dumb, old church.*"

Chapter Twenty-One

The next afternoon, Christopher and Paul Wolenski were on a plane destined for Denver, with a continuation on to Colorado Springs.

Paul Wolenski, or Pauli, as he was called, had become Christopher's right hand man over the past six months.

Pauli was a big, tough sort of guy, but not all that bright, academically. Originally from the Chicago area, he had come out to Northern Cal on a football scholarship.

After flunking out of school, he had hung around the little college town adjacent to the university, working as a waiter in the restaurant below the church.

Like so many others, he was drawn to Brad Hawkins like a magnet.

Pauli was just the sort of fellow Christopher needed to work behind the lines, so to speak. In addition to being big and tough, he was also very loyal and thorough to carry out assignments.

After landing in Colorado Springs, they rented a four wheel drive, off-road vehicle, and spent a little time studying an area road map.

Making their way through the city, they eventually started up Highway 24, passing through the little town of Manitou Springs, and passing by Pike's Peak on the left.

Several hours later, approximately half way between Colorado Springs and Aspen; about five miles past the little mountain village of Roper; they turned left onto a little dirt road in the Pike National Forest area.

Three quarters of a mile up the little dirt road, and there was the ranch right before them. Momma Elsie's directions were *"right on the button."*

The ranch was a bit run down, and a few illegal squatters had taken up residency on the property, but Christopher could see the potential.

There was a large, roomy, main house; two sizeable bunk houses; a huge barn; two storage type buildings; and an old fashioned, hand pump, artesian well with an endless supply of good, cold, mountain water.

Back in their rented, off-road vehicle, Christopher and Pauli spent several hours traversing the entire property.

There was ample pasture land, but quite a lot of work necessary to repair the fences.

There were beautiful rolling hills with rugged peaks in the background; and a cold, rushing stream plummeting out of the high mountains, and running right through the middle of the property.

"It's perfect," exclaimed Christopher, *"Absolutely perfect!"*

Back in San Francisco the next Monday morning, Christopher and Momma Elsie were seated in the plush conference room of the law offices of Dothard and Hutch.

Christopher looked a little out of place in his corduroy parka, sandals, jeans and blond dreadlocks falling over his shoulders.

His appearance didn't go unnoticed by the curious parade of girls from the secretarial pool, who just happened to be passing by the conference room!

Mr. Amos Dothard, the senior partner of the law firm was noticeably reluctant, but eventually yielded to Momma Elsie's firm wishes.

Before breaking for lunch, He guided them through the process of signing paperwork which legally transferred ownership of the ranch to Bradley Eugene Hawkins.

After completing their business, Christopher waited outside Mr. Dothard's office, while he and Momma Elsie discussed some of her other financial matters.

He could easily see them through the intricately carved, glass window in the upper half of the office door. Almost certainly, Mr. Dothard was cautioning Momma Elsie about her involvement with him.

He wondered just how much this old woman was worth?

Book Three

The Promised Land

"Then if anyone says to you, look, here is the Christ! Or there! Do not believe it.....If they say to you, look, He is in the desert! Do not go out; or look, he is in the inner rooms! Do not believe it."

>Jesus Christ
>The Gospel According to Matthew
>Chapter 24, verses 23 & 26

Chapter Twenty-Two

A little over one month later, they were ready for the move to Colorado.

However, during this time of packing and preparing for the move, the church had lost about 50 additional people. After the initial emotion had worn off, the reality of leaving the conveniences of the big city had set in, influencing the least committed.

There was a big push to raise money. Due to the low overhead of the church, and due to the generosity of several members, Christopher had managed to save almost $200,000.00, but he could foresee the need for considerably more money.

Consequently, right up to the actual day of departure, there was a great emphasis on sacrificial giving.

Momma Elsie sold her home of many years and gave the entire proceeds to the church. Several other older members also gave sizeable gifts.

In addition to these special offerings, there were all kinds of garage sales, yard sales, bake sales and every other type of fund raiser that would bring in finances.

By departure time, the church had more than half a million dollars!

The first week in July, they officially began their move. Around 300 souls leaving behind the corruption, pollution, violence, injustice, and in general, the fast paced life of the big city; going off to find their utopia, their promised land, their heaven on earth; led by a spoiled, self-centered, 23 year old, would be messiah!

Christopher, Pauli, Naomi and Momma Elsie traveled by plane.

Several groups chartered buses.

Others drove cars, mini-vans and pick-up trucks, loaded down with a variety of household items, food, clothing, and lots of camping equipment.

Most went directly to Colorado. A few visited family or friends on the way, but everyone was there by the middle of July.

As each new group arrived at the ranch, there were stories to tell. Mostly, these were stories about how family members or friends tried to discourage them from coming, and how they overcame these attempts from the enemy!

Initially, the new community was just a huge *"tent city."* It was one, big, camping out experience.

During the day, there was time for a quick, and rather stimulating bath in one of the pools formed by the cold rushing stream that cascaded out of the high mountains.

There was a continual aroma in the air from the constant cooking on a multitude of bar-be-que grills.

And, at night, there was curling up in a nice warm sleeping bag under a sky full of stars.

For most of them, it was the happiest, and most wonderful time of their lives!

Even Momma Elsie and the small number of older church members were having a great time. The younger kids looked upon them as their grandparents, and went out of their way to take special care of them.

Christopher immediately turned the big barn into the assembly hall.

Every morning, they gathered to hear about the daily tasks to be completed, and to receive their individual work assignments.

And at night, they gathered for singing, testimonies, and spiritual instruction.

It was during one of the evening gatherings, about one week after they arrived, that Christopher made a significant announcement.

"We are no longer The Church of the Open Heart," he explained. *"In fact, we are not a church at all. We are a community, a family! From this day forth, we shall be called: The Family of God!"*

Chapter Twenty-Three

The next four months were a *"bee hive"* of activity. There was considerable work to be accomplished before the cold, and often harsh winter season.

Almost daily, trucks were traveling into Colorado Springs and returning in the afternoons loaded with lumber, paint, cement and other building supplies. The air was filled with the buzz of saws and the hammering of nails.

The bunk houses and storage buildings were renovated and refurbished into living quarters, and subsequently sectioned into individual living cubicles.

The main house was repaired, painted and turned into Family of God headquarters as well as Christopher's private living quarters.

The outside of the barn was repaired and painted. The inside was restructured and insulated in order to provide a more suitable meeting hall.

Almost everyday, Family of God members were visiting farms throughout the area, and returning with huge amounts of farm fresh vegetables, fruit, honey and other food stuffs.

A large number of the women worked among a *"sea"* of mason jars, canning and preserving foods.

Wood chopping expeditions were sent out, and subsequently, stacks of fire wood grew as high as the roofs of the buildings. Wood burning stoves were purchased and installed in the living quarters.

There were teams assigned to spend the bulk of their day harvesting the cold, mountain streams. They would return at the end of the day with their lines full of mountain trout.

Some of the men canvassed the area in their pick-up trucks, looking for used stoves, refrigerators, and other appliances. Several large, deep freezers were obtained, and they quickly filled up with fish as well as beef, chicken, lamb and deer from other farms and ranches in the area.

Solar panels were placed on the roofs of buildings, and subsequently, hot water heaters were installed.

Several windmills were erected to provide an additional source of energy in order to limit their dependence upon the outside world.

And, there was the constant preparation and cooking of food, followed by the ever popular KP duty. It was quite a task to feed 300 people, three times a day.

But, these were good times. Everyone had their individual assignments, and for the most part, the community worked together as a unit.

There was a cause; a purpose for their lives. Nobody even considered, much less examined the possibility that they might be involved in a cult.

Of course, there were a few disgruntled people in the group. Mostly, it was people who didn't want to work. Christopher adeptly used the Bible to address these problems, *"....if anyone will not work, neither shall he eat."* There were a dozen or so who were eventually asked to leave.

Occasionally, there was a disagreement or personality clash among the people. Consequently, Christopher formed a 12 person judicial council, consisting of members from a cross section of the Family.

And then, there was Paul Wolenski, who was appointed as judge!

Christopher took advantage of this time of harmony to ingrain his spiritual philosophy into the people.

There was still some teaching from the Bible, but most of the teaching these days was from Christopher's recently acquired personal library. Books on such subjects as metaphysics, spiritism and mind science. The visitation had a greater influence on his life than anyone realized.

During one of the evening meetings, Christopher announced another significant change.

"We will no longer refer to this place as The Bar 7 Ranch. From this day forth, this property will officially be called: The Promised Land."

The Family of God was slowly being molded and manipulated into *"sold out"* disciples of Christopher Judah.

And, in the process, they were being drawn deeper and deeper into the grasp of deception.

"But there were also false prophets among the people, even as there will be false teachers among you, WHO WILL SECRETLY BRING IN DESTRUCTIVE HERESIES."

Second Epistle of the Apostle Peter
Chapter 2, verse 1

Chapter Twenty-Four

Very early, one frosty morning, about two weeks before Christmas, the little community was rudely awakened by the blaring of sirens, the flashing of lights, and someone barking out commands through one of those battery powered megaphones.

As everyone sleepily filed out of the main house, the bunkhouses and other living quarters; shivering in the morning cold; they discovered that their compound was semi-surrounded by 15 law enforcement vehicles.

At least 30 officers crouched behind their vehicles, armed with assault rifles and shotguns.

As the Family of God whispered among themselves as to what was happening, an imposing figure cautiously emerged from the perimeter.

Sheriff Arlan Prichard was, to put it mildly, a *"tough old bird."* At six feet, four inches tall, around 230 pounds, he was still *"hardnosed"* and burly at 50 years of age.

He had served for ten years as county sheriff after a 22 year career in the Marine Corps.

"Who's in charge of this here outfit," barked Sheriff Prichard; his face partially hidden by a thick, graying mustache, aviator sun glasses and one of those drill instructor type hats.

"Have you come out, as against a robber, with swords and clubs," Christopher answered, quoting Jesus from the Garden of Gethsemane?

"Don't get smart with me, son," warned Sheriff Prichard, pointing a thick finger in Christopher's direction. *"I didn't know what to expect up here. For all we knew, this was another one of those David Koresh things! Is this some kind of a cult?"*

"Let me assure you, sheriff; uh, I'm sorry, I didn't get your name?"

"I didn't give it, son, but it's Prichard. Sheriff Arlan Prichard."

"Well, you can relax, Sheriff Prichard. I can assure you that the Family of God is a peace loving community.

"We mean no harm to anyone, and we sincerely hope no one means any harm to us. So, Sheriff, what is the problem?"

"Well, son, I've been getting a few complaints."

"Complaints, sheriff? Have we been disturbing our distant neighbors with our music and singing, or something?"

"Naw, nothing like that. I'm talking about complaints from some of the parents of the kids up here. They claim they haven't received any mail; and for all they know, the mail they sent hasn't been delivered either. After all, son, it is the Christmas season!"

"I can assure you, sheriff, that all mail had been delivered; and no one has been hindered from writing, nor hindered in anyway from contacting their relatives."

Sheriff Prichard mused over the situation for a few moments, looking around the compound, then scrutinizing the Family of God.

Christopher kept right on talking, *"but I will tell you this much, sheriff. Here in the Family of God, we live on a higher spiritual dimension. Our priorities are different. We don't have time for the nonsense and sentimentality of the outside world. We're about the business of God up here."*

Sheriff Prichard raised his eyebrows, looked at one of his deputies, and then back at Christopher. *"I assume that you're the leader of this bunch?"*

"Christopher Judah at your service, Sheriff Prichard." He extended his hand in Arlan Prichard's direction.

For a long few moments, Arlan Prichard extended an icy stare at Christopher, not bothering to accept his hand.

"Christopher Judah, huh? What's your real name, son?"

"The name I was given is Christopher Judah, and I am the spiritual leader of the Family of God."

"Well, son," Arlan Prichard concluded, "whoever you are, and whatever your name is; I sincerely hope you never provide me with the occasion to come up here with anything more serious than today's visit!"

Then, with a wave of his hand, the deputies lowered their weapons and retreated to their vehicles. Within minutes, they had vacated the property.

Chapter Twenty-Five

The Family of God endured a bitterly cold winter. Despite the weather conditions, the daily chores still had to be completed.

In addition, there was an ongoing need to upgrade the living quarters, making them more liveable and warmer.

Consequently, due to harsh conditions, there began to be a grumbling among the people.

To maintain control, Christopher altered his tactics of spiritual instruction. He incorrectly used scriptures out of their context, making them seem to apply to the people's loyalty.

He used inapplicable scriptures to warn them of the dangers of leaving the Promised Land, *"Blessed are those who do his commandments, that they may have the right to the tree of life, and may enter through the gates into the city. But outside are dogs and sorcerers and sexually immoral and murderers and idolaters, and whoever loves and practices a lie."*

The spiritual instruction could be described as a clever combination of fear and loving care.

And, more and more, Christopher openly referred to himself as their messiah, and the Family of God as the only people who were not lost!

The coming of Spring perked up the countenance and attitudes of the people. The snow disappeared; the thick layer of ice in the rushing stream began to break up; and wild flowers began to pop out on the mountain sides.

This prompted a new, energetic project for the Family of God. They had managed to get one of the old tractors working, and one of the plows repaired. Thus, they began to turn the soil.

This was followed by mass plantings of squash, beans, tomatoes, corn, strawberries, watermelon and any other kind of vegetable or fruit that would grow in the area.

This should have offered Christopher some relief from his hard preaching, but now he had another pressing problem. The Family of God was running out of money!

What started out as more than half a million dollars had now dwindled down to around $25,000.00. It was extremely expensive to operate and maintain a community like the Promised Land.

Late at night, Christopher wandered through the halls of the main house, worrying about, and trying to figure out how to raise more money.

Thus began a new round of preaching on the willingness to give up everything for the sake of the Family of God and their Promised Land.

Christopher was certain the people still had money stashed away in bank accounts, just in case this utopia didn't work out.

One by one, the guilt began to affect the people. They brought jewelry; all but a select few sold the vehicles they had brought with them; and most importantly, those secret bank accounts were emptied and the money brought to Christopher.

Also, during this period of time, new people began to join the little community. Now that Winter had passed, and Spring was in full bloom, it was more convenient to seek out a messiah. By the beginning of Summer, the Family of God had grown to around 325 souls.

Of course, these new converts were thoroughly instructed about the importance of giving their all as a prerequisite for joining the Family of God.

As a result of all these efforts, their bank account slowly increased until their assets climbed back over $100,000.00.

But, Christopher wasn't content. *"When this money runs out, then what,"* he thought to himself? *"I suppose we could farm out some hired help to the surrounding farms and ranches. Maybe we could sell some of the produce we're growing?"* He continued to worry about finances.

One early Summer morning, Momma Elsie popped into the office.

Christopher's countenance cheered up. *"Maybe she's brought a special offering,"* he hoped?

"Momma Elsie, how are you, and what can I do for you this bright, sunshiny morning?"

"I'm doing very well, thank you. Now, Christopher, I need to discuss something very important with you. You know that I trust you. I look upon you as my own son, especially since I haven't heard a word from my actual children in more than three years. And, you also know, Christopher, that I consider the Family of God as my very own family.

Well, for the past several months I've been thinking about the Family's need for more finances."

She paused momentarily. *"Well, I seem to be getting ahead of myself. There's something else I need to say before I continue."*

"Christopher," she continued, *"I have decided that I want to live out the remainder of my days right here in the Promised Land. Coming back to this place where Daniel and I had so many good years has brought back pleasant memories. And, I'm so pleased at the way you've fixed up the place!"*

A tear streamed down Momma Elsie's aged face.

"Momma Elsie, I can't begin to tell you what a blessing, what an inspiration you have been to all of us." Christopher moved over to the sofa beside Momma Elsie, put an arm around her, and placed a kiss on her forehead.

"Thank you," sobbed Momma Elsie, as she paused to blow her nose and wipe her eyes.

"Well, Christopher," she continued, *"I have come to a decision. Yesterday, when I went down to the village, I telephoned Mr. Dothard, my lawyer back in San Francisco. Oh, he tried to talk me out of it, but I was persistent with him. Anyway, I've instructed him to change my will. I'm leaving everything to you, Christopher, for the Family of God!"*

Christopher struggled to contain his excitement and act surprised. *"I'm just flabbergasted, Momma Elsie. I had no idea, I don't know what to say!"*

Actually, he had laid awake at nights scheming about how he could continue to tap into this old woman's wealth.

Within three weeks, the paperwork had arrived at the compound via registered mail. The will was signed, notarized and returned to the law offices of Dothard and Hutch.

"But there were false prophets also among the people, even as there shall be false teachers among you....and through covetousness shall they with feigned *(artificial)* words MAKE MERCHANDISE OF YOU...." (KJV).

Second Epistle of the Apostle Peter
From Chapter 2, verses 1 & 3

Chapter Twenty-Six

From his makeshift, adjacent office in the main house, Pauli had secretly listened to the conversation between Momma Elsie and Christopher.

Over the next several weeks, he spent a lot of time thinking about the matter. Now that the will had officially been changed, he approached Christopher. They were discussing the situation.

"How much do you figure the old girl's worth," quipped Pauli?

"Don't know," answered Christopher, "but if her past giving is any indication, then it's likely that she's worth a bundle!"

"Well then, my next question is, how long do you think we'll have to wait to find out?"

"Don't know that either. She's old, just made 80, but she seems to be robust and in rather good health."

There were several minutes of silence between them until Pauli spoke up again, "we could speed up the process."

Christopher had a puzzled look on his face. "What in the world are you talking about," he asked?

"Just what I said. We could speed up the process of her inevitable death. She's an old woman. She's outlived her usefulness. Have you seen how the kids dote over her, waiting on her hand and foot?"

"Pauli," Christopher interrupted, "I'm not sure I want to hear anymore...!"

"Listen, Christopher," Pauli pressed the issue. "Her money would be of much greater value to the Family of God, than would her continued, and possibly prolonged presence."

"So, what do you suggest we do, go out and knife her or something? There are laws against murder, you know!"

"My dear Christopher, there are ways that these things can be done that won't even leave a clue as to what happened."

Christopher contemplated the matter before responding, "Isn't this what they call Euthanasia?"

"*Eutha what,*" replied Pauli, showing his lack of academic prowess?

"*Euthanasia,*" answered Christopher. "*It's the practice of killing individuals who are hopelessly sick or injured. It can also apply to the elimination of aged people who are a burden to society?*"

"*Well, I don't understand all your 50 cent words, Christopher. You can call it by whatever name you like, but the fact is, we would have her money!*"

"*The consequences would be grave if we were caught,*" Christopher responded. "*Are you sure that you can do it in such a way that no one would suspect us?*"

Pauli displayed a cold, but confident grin before answering, "*Christopher, you can trust me on this one!*"

Christopher stood up, walked slowly into the kitchen, poured himself a cup of tea, and walked back into the office.

There was a momentary question as to whether he was struggling with the concept of good verses evil; or just weighing the benefits of having either Momma Elsie or her money.

"*Pauli,*" he finally responded, "*I must reemphasize; There can't be any suspicion whatsoever of any wrongdoing. And, I'm not just talking about suspicion from law enforcement officers. I especially don't want there to be any suspicion from Family of God members!*"

From that day, Pauli, in a very calculated and cold manner, began to gradually add arsenic to Momma Elsie's food.

By the beginning of Autumn, she was dead!

"Beware of false prophets, who come to you in sheep's clothing, but inwardly they are ravenous wolves."

Jesus Christ
The Gospel According to Matthew
Chapter 7, verse 15

Chapter Twenty-Seven

There was great grief in the Family of God. No one could explain Momma Elsie's sudden illness. She was such a picture of vibrant health. Even after she became ill, everyone was sure she would recover.

In his usual cunning manner, Christopher came up with some sterling messages of consolation.

Several days after Momma Elsie was buried, one of the children in the Family of God asked a challenging question, *"Christopher, where is Momma Elsie now? Is she in heaven, or hell, or what?"*

"I'm glad you asked that question, little sister," Christopher lied. *"You'll be happy to know that this Sunday's message deals with that very subject."*

Actually, Christopher didn't have a clue about the hereafter. He was too busy building his kingdom here on earth. He didn't even know if there was any such place as heaven, or whatever you wanted to call it. In a few short days, however, he would have to come up with an answer!

For the next several days, he furiously read and studied his religious books. It was difficult to create a doctrine on something you knew absolutely nothing about. Nevertheless, by Sunday, he was ready to answer the people's questions.

"There are many paths that lead to God," he began. *"Throughout the annals of history, God has raised up messiahs from different cultural and geographical backgrounds to lead his people to that ultimate promised land, which some call heaven. It makes no difference what you call that eternal resting place. What's important is how you get there!*

Many messiahs, although they were truly chosen by God, ultimately failed to fulfill what they were chosen to do. I've explained to you about the failure of Jesus Christ; and all of you are knowledgeable concerning the more recent failures of Jim Jones and David Koresh.

Now, God has chosen me to be your messiah, and I assure you, I will not fail! Therefore, those of you who have wholeheartedly chosen to follow me will not fail to reach that eternal promised land.

I can't answer for those who have gone out from among us. I fear that their eternal souls are doomed to wander forever.

As I have explained to you many times, God called us out from the corruption, pollution, violence, degradation, moral filth and injustice of the world; and here in our temporary promised land, we are becoming more like God.

As we learn, and as we grow, we gradually take on more and more of the nature and character of God. Thus, we are preparing ourselves for that eternal promised land where we will live forever in the presence of God.

We must strive within ourselves to be godlike. I'm talking about our attitudes and actions; loving, accepting, respecting and being kind to one another.

I can assure you that Momma Elsie has gone on to her reward in that eternal promised land. All of you know how caring, how loving and unselfish she was.

Just as trees and plants absorb oxygen through the process of osmosis, Momma Elsie, during her time among us, became as the very essence of the character and nature of God!"

There were a few questions, but for the most part, everyone appeared to be satisfied with this seemingly logical analysis and explanation.

As they intently listened to the message that morning, many of them, either publicly or privately, made fresh, new commitments to the Family of God, and to Christopher Judah as their messiah.

They determined within themselves that they would achieve this level of godlikeness described by their messiah.

They too, would strive to be worthy of that eternal promised land.

"There is a way which seems right to a man, but its end is the way of death."

The Wisdom of King Solomon
Proverbs, Chapter 14, verse 12

Chapter Twenty-Eight

About two weeks after Momma Elsie passed away, Christopher returned to San Francisco to claim his inheritance.

He left Pauli in charge, explaining to the Family of God that he had to take care of some business relating to Momma Elsie's death.

Just after Momma Elsie died, Christopher had located an old, county coroner in the village of Roper. Of course, there was no need for an autopsy. Just an old woman who had lived out her years and peacefully passed away. Within a couple of days, he had the death certificate in hand.

She was buried on a little grassy knoll overlooking that beautiful, rushing stream which ran through the property. She always said it was her favorite spot, even in earlier times when she and her husband were running the ranch.

While going through Momma Elsie's personal belongings, Christopher discovered that she had two sons and one daughter. He knew she had children, but didn't know how many, nor their whereabouts.

He discovered that the oldest son and the daughter were living in Europe. The son lived in Germany where he had married a wife during his military career. The daughter lived in Greece. It was a bit unclear as to what she was doing?

The younger son was somewhere in the South Pacific on a sailing yacht.

Christopher didn't even attempt to contact the children. Late one night, after the compound had settled down, he burned all her personal papers in one of the 50 gallon drums they used for an incinerator.

Now, once again, here was Bradley Eugene Hawkins, alias Christopher Judah, seated in the cushy law offices of Dothard and Hutch.

He had requested of Momma Elsie, that she put the will in his legal name to avoid any complications.

And, this was a different Brad Hawkins than the one Mr. Dothard had encountered previously. The dread locks were gone, he was clean shaven and dressed in a suit and tie.

"Well, Mr. Hawkins, everything seems to be in order. Mrs. Thompson had liquidated everything except her cash holdings, so executing the will was rather simple. How did you say she died?"

"Just old age, Mr. Dothard. As you know, she was 80 years old."

"Yes, I know. It just seems that she died rather quickly after changing her will."

"Mr. Dothard, I believe she knew in her heart that her time was soon. She was just getting her affairs in order."

"Yes, well, Mr. Hawkins, here's a check drawn on the Bay Area First National Bank. All the appropriate fees have been taken out, so this officially settles her estate."

"Thank you very kindly, Mr. Dothard, and please have a pleasant day."

About half an hour later, Brad was enjoying some fresh oysters, pasta and sourdough bread at one of the finer restaurants in the Fisherman's Wharf area.

He gingerly opened the fancy envelope and peeked inside. He could hardly contain his excitement as his eyes fell upon a check made out to: Bradley Eugene Hawkins, for an amount just exceeding one million, four hundred thousand dollars!

Before returning to the Promised Land and the Family of God, he purchased himself a brand new, luxury model, four wheel drive, off-road vehicle with all the extras.

Then, he spent a little time hitting the bars and picking up a few girls. *"I guess a small amount of corruption and a small amount of pollution never hurt anyone,"* he chuckled to himself!

Chapter Twenty-Nine

Maria Mendoza was an exceptionally pretty, 17 year old, Spanish girl; who, until recently, had lived with her family just south of San Diego.

On this particular day, however, her beauty wasn't exactly shining through. She was tired, hungry and depressed as she sat on the curb outside the Colorado Springs bus station; clutching a few possessions in her hands.

Maria was the type of girl that required a lot of affection and attention. Being the first of nine children, she rarely received any of that needed affection or attention at home.

As the oldest child, she was constantly required to care for her younger brothers and sisters while her mother worked two jobs to keep the family clothed and fed.

Then, there was her father. She certainly didn't receive any attention or affection from him. He followed the trail of migrant farm workers that extended from California to Washington, so he was rarely at home.

It was just over a month now that Maria had become enamored with a young rodeo star passing through San Diego. He paid her a little attention, followed by a little affection. She had subsequently made an impulsive decision to run off with him.

For a while, they had a wonderful time. Every night, she was with this handsome, young cowboy as he rode the broncos in every little town between San Diego and Colorado Springs.

After performances, a whole gang of them would stay up until the wee hours of the morning, laughing, singing, telling exaggerated stories, getting saturated on cheap beer; and then sleeping it off until time for the next night's performance.

In time, however, her so-called knight in shining armor had grown tired of her, and had unceremoniously dumped her.

Now, here she was, sitting on the curb outside the Colorado Springs bus station, depressed, tired, hungry, and without so much as one thin dime in her pocket.

On that same day, David Palmer was on his way into Colorado Springs. He had been given the responsibility to periodically make these trips to pick up special supplies which could not be obtained from the small towns near the compound. He was one of the few members of the Family of God who still had their own personal vehicle.

David was also an original member of the group as far back as the Bible study at Northern California University.

He had this strong need for a messiah figure in his life. Consequently, he had eagerly followed Christopher to Colorado, dragging along his somewhat reluctant wife, Cindy.

It was because he was considered trustworthy and loyal, that he had been given this special responsibility to make these shopping trips into Colorado Springs.

On this particular day, however, David was troubled inside. He didn't understand about Momma Elsie's death. One day, she was the picture of health, and shortly thereafter, she was dead. They just kept saying it was a virus, and she would get over it. They didn't even call a doctor!

Also, rumors had been floating around the Promised Land about Momma Elsie's will. Not from Christopher and Pauli! They were always tightlipped and secretive about business matters. On the other hand, Naomi was a little more likely to let things slip out.

He had always been extremely committed to Christopher Judah, but he was beginning to wonder if there was more to Momma Elsie's death than just an old woman passing away in the fullness of her years.
His thoughts were temporarily interrupted as he spotted a distraught looking young girl seated on the curb by the bus station.
He pulled his old, beat up, 1978, pickup over to the curb.
"Excuse me, you look like you could use a friend."
Maria started to cry.
"Hey, don't cry, everything's going to be all right." He handed her an apple, which she eagerly devoured.
"You waiting for a bus?"
"Not really, I have no money."
"Where you from?"
"San Diego, but I don't think I can go back there!"
"Listen, my name is David Palmer. I'm part of a group called the Family of God. We have a compound called the Promised Land up in the mountains. If you really don't have anywhere to go, you could hang out with us for a few days."
"Thank you very much. My name is Maria Mendoza, and that's the best offer I received today."

Chapter Thirty

Christopher noticed Maria the first day she arrived at the Promised Land. He went out of his way to give her special attention; supposedly caring for a wounded member of the outside world who had been rescued by the Family of God.

The truth was, his attention was mostly motivated by lust!

And Maria, she was thoroughly enjoying all this attention. This was exactly what she needed. In her usual naive and gullible manner, she thought Christopher was the most wonderful person in the whole world. He could do no wrong!

He had openly welcomed her into the Family of God. He had spent special time with her, counseling her, and supposedly helping her to overcome the hurts she had experienced.

She was sure that he was the most compassionate and caring man alive. Perhaps he was a messiah!

About two months after Maria arrived, Christopher called her into his office one day. He had laid awake at nights, thinking about her, desiring to have her.

As for Maria, she thought maybe this was some additional follow-up counseling.

"Good afternoon, Maria, and how are you this fine day?"

"Oh, just fine, thank you very much."

"I hope you're enjoying your time here in the Promised Land. Is there anything you need?"

"No, I don't need anything. Everyone here is treating me so wonderful."

Maria was back to her usually bubbly self. "Christopher," she exclaimed, "you are like the father I was never close to, and like the priest I could never approach!"

"Maria, it pleases me to hear you say that."

He hesitated for a few moments before continuing, "Maria, I'm hoping that we can become even closer friends?"

"Well, O.K., sure, but I don't know how....?"

Christopher cut her off in the middle of the sentence. *"Maria, God has given me the enormous task of being a messiah, a spiritual leader to the people here in the Family of God. Sometimes the task is stressful and demanding. Even though I've been chosen by God, I sometimes need the emotional comfort that only a woman like yourself can provide."*

"I don't understand?"

Christopher again hesitated for a few moments, and then came right out with the proposition, *"Maria, I need for you to be my woman."*

Maria had a confused look on her face. *"I don't understand, Christopher. Are you asking me to marry you? To be your wife, or something?"*

"Well, yes, I suppose you could put it that way."

"I don't know what to say, Christopher! This is so sudden! I'm very surprised! Will we be having a wedding? Are we going to be married by a priest?"

"Maria, I'm a little disappointed in you. I was hoping by now, that you would have become more enlightened. Don't you realize that weddings and other such ceremonies are just creations of society, and in reality, they are a meaningless and worthless waste of time?"

"I didn't know, I always thought...."
He again cut her off in the middle of a sentence. *"Don't you remember, Maria, in the Bible it says that men took unto themselves, wives?"*
Maria didn't remember any such thing. Of course, she really didn't know what was, or was not in the Bible. The little she knew about the Bible, she heard from her priest. Whatever he said, she just took his word for it.
In a similar manner, she guessed that whatever Christopher said must be right.
She sat there for a few minutes, struggling in her mind, but not being able to find an opposing response to his calculated and persuasive approach. Even though she was looking down at the floor, she could feel his constant gaze!
She had always been weak, and seemingly never able to say no! Consequently, she had been taken advantage of more than once.
"Maybe it will be different this time," she thought. *"After all, he is a man of God!"*
Christopher pressed the issue, *"so what is your answer, Maria? Will you accept the offer to become my woman? Will you take care of me as I care for the Family of God?"*
Maria didn't want to take care of someone else! She wanted someone to take care of her, but she was unable to come up with an argument.

She felt herself weakening, and running out of excuses. *"Well, O.K., I guess. If you really believe it's the right thing to do!"*

"Maria, I know it's right. I believe you are God's gift to me!"

There was no backing out now. It was too late. She felt vulnerable and victimized as Christopher took her hand and led her into his bedroom.

As Maria was slowly and reluctantly undressing, she detected a change in Christopher's eyes.

Gone was the look of compassion and care she had experienced since the day she arrived.

In its place, there seemed to be the eyes of a conqueror, gloating over his conquest!

"But there were also false prophets among the people, even as there will be false teachers among you....HAVING EYES FULL OF ADULTERY AND THAT CANNOT CEASE FROM SIN...."

Second Epistle of the Apostle Peter
From Chapter 2, verses 1 & 14

Chapter Thirty-One

It seemed that Christopher's personality changed after he returned from San Francisco. He was becoming more paranoid, thinking that everyone was out to get him!

Strangely enough, he was still concerned about finances, even though the Family of God now had more than one and a half million dollars in assets.

The Family didn't notice these changes. As always, he was a good actor. But, they did notice a new twist in his teaching.

He spent more time lambasting government officials from the national level to the local level, criticizing what he perceived as corruption and injustice.

The compound's only television set was in Christopher's private room. Most of the people had sold their personal vehicles, thus limiting their access to the outside world; so Christopher decided that he would tell the Family of God what they needed to know.

Consequently, he watched a lot of news broadcasts, gathering material to keep the people informed from his slanted viewpoint.

Unfortunately, Christopher continued to become more and more paranoid, not just about money, but about politics as well.

He became convinced that the United States government would imminently suffer a financial collapse. His teaching frequently contained warnings and predictions of doom and gloom.

Of course, the Family of God echoed their amens. They were all snug and secure, isolated and protected from the horrors of the outside world.

As the Family of God was preparing for their second winter in the Promised Land, Christopher made a bizarre decision.

For several months leading up to the first of the year, he made a number of trips into Denver, often under hazardous driving conditions.

He was secretly meeting with a Denver based brokerage house, and privately turning the Family's assets into gold!

There were gold bars of various sizes and weights. There were numerous gold coins struck at mints in Canada, Mexico and South Africa as well as the United States. There were even some valuable antique gold coins.

Slowly but surely, the entire assets of the Family of God, more than one and a half million dollars was being turned into gold.

A large, double locking, combination safe was quietly delivered and installed in Christopher's office. Besides himself, only Pauli knew the combinations.

Yet, despite this apparent increase in security from the world's monetary systems, he continued to worry about money. His paranoia was bordering on greed!

The Family of God began to sell firewood to some of the more upscale neighbors in the area.

They marketed some of their preserved foods under the label: PROMISED LAND NATURAL AND ORGANIC FOODS.

They occasionally farmed out teams of workers to assist other farms and ranches in the area.

They even cut and sold Christmas trees from their property. Anything to make more money!

As a result, their assets continued to increase. There was very little overhead these days. They had worked hard toward becoming a totally self-sufficient community.

Of course, when cash assets built up to a certain level, Christopher continued to turn them into gold.

More than ever, he was convinced; in fact, thought he had heard from God regarding an imminent financial collapse of the United States government. He was determined that he would not be a part of, nor affected by a failed monetary system.

Consequently, he continued to preach about the ills of the government, criticizing officials at all levels. He wrote so-called, prophetic letters to politicians at the local, state and national level, warning them of an imminent collapse of the government.

Subsequently, he wrote letters for the editorial pages of local newspapers, prophesying the downfall of the same politicians for not heeding his warnings.

At the same time, he continued to reinforce the deceptive security blanket he had carefully wrapped around the Family of God.

"But there were also false prophets among the people, even as there will be false teachers among you....THEY ARE NOT AFRAID TO SPEAK EVIL OF DIGNITARIES."

Second Epistle of the Apostle Peter
From Chapter 2, verses 1 & 10

Chapter Thirty-Two

"*Christopher, I must talk to you,*" Maria was sheepishly and apologetically peering into Christopher's office.

She received a glaring, unsympathetic look from Naomi.

"*What do you want now,*" asked Christopher, showing his impatience? "*Can't you see that I'm very busy?*"

"*You're always busy, but I must talk to you!*"

"*Can't it wait until later, Maria?*"

"*No, Christopher, it can't wait for later. I've been trying to talk to you for days, and you always say later!*"

"O.K., O.K., what is it?"

"I must talk with you in private."

Christopher reluctantly pushed aside his work, and with irritation in his voice, said, "all right, hurry up, get in here. I don't have all day!"

As he closed the office door, he noticed a look of fear on Maria's face.

"I'm pregnant."

"What do you mean, pregnant? How, when?"

"You already know how."

"What I mean, Maria," there was a note of sarcasm in his voice, "is how long have you been pregnant?"

"About ten weeks, I think. I'm not completely sure."

"And, why haven't you told me about this before now?" Christopher was visibly angry.

"I was afraid."

"Afraid! Afraid of what?"

"I was afraid you would get angry at me." She was noticeably trembling.

"Well, you're right about that! I'm very upset and definitely angry! Do you know how dangerous it is to bring a child into the world these days? A world that is filled with corruption, pollution, violence and injustice! A world that is completely out of control!"

Maria started to cry.

"Maria," Christopher raised his voice at her, "stop that silly whimpering!"

Maria blew her nose, wiped her eyes and tried to stop crying.

"Christopher," she explained, her voice periodically interrupted by sobs, *"there are children here in the Promised Land. Our child could grow up right here and be safe."*

"You don't understand anything, Maria. I have tremendous responsibilities, caring for all the members of the Family of God. I don't have time for a child. You should have been more careful!"

"I'll take care of the child, Christopher. You won't have to be worried about it. I've had lots of experience taking care of my sisters and brothers."

Christopher paced around the office for a few minutes as if he didn't hear Maria's last statement.

Finally he spoke, *"you'll have to have an abortion!"*

"No, Christopher! Please, no! Please don't make me do this! I just can't do it!"

"The matter is settled, Maria. You will have an abortion, and I don't want to hear anymore about it!"

Now Maria really started to cry, uncontrollably. Everything in her Catholic background screamed out against this decision that was being forced upon her, but she was too weak to object.

"Shut up, Maria, just shut up," snapped Christopher. *"And, you better not breathe a word of this to anybody."*

139

After hustling Maria out of the office, he momentarily stopped at Naomi's desk before returning to his office. *"And you better not breathe a word about this to anybody either!"*

Several days later, sometime during the middle of the night, Pauli's big, black, pickup truck; noisily idling; eased as quietly as possible out of the compound, headed for an abortion clinic.

Maria sat submissively on the passenger side. She was quiet on the outside, but crying on the inside. She didn't dare say anything. She was more afraid of Pauli than she was of Christopher.

Chapter Thirty-Three

One day, about two weeks after Maria's abortion, Christopher was in Denver on one of his clandestine conversion trips, turning cash into gold.

Naomi took advantage of the situation to seek out Maria. In her sassy sort of way, she sarcastically tormented her, *"So, what's it like being Christopher's woman?"*

"What? How do you know about that?" Maria looked betrayed.

"Well, for crying out loud, Maria, don't look so shocked! Everybody in the Promised Land knows you're Christopher's latest whore!"

Maria looked bewildered. She was at a loss for words.

Naomi continued to mock her, *"Oh, I'm so sorry! Did you think you were the only one? Well, I've got big news for you, sister. I used to be his woman, before you came along; and there have been others too!"*

"I didn't know!"

"Maria, honey, you are one gullible, naive child."

Later that day, Maria was alone, out in the area which Family of God members called Clingman's Cliff.

It was a beautiful, but treacherous area. A large, flat rock, jutting out into the sky like a diving board; which then overlooked a steep and sudden drop into a deep, narrow ravine.

Family of God members liked to come up here in the evenings to relax and enjoy the rugged, natural beauty; but they were careful not to get to close to the edge of the cliff.

As evening disappeared into nightfall, Maria sat perilously close to the edge of the cliff. There was a war being waged in her mind.

"Maybe I should leave the Family of God," she softly mumbled to herself, tears freely streaming down her face. *"Maybe I should just go back home to San Diego."*

"No," she continued, "I could never go back home again. I deserted my brothers and sisters. My father would not accept me back!"

"And, I know for sure that he would not accept me back if he knew the horrible thing that I did!"

She quietly sobbed for a while; then began talking to herself again.

"He never even said it was a child. He just called it a fetus, and tissue that had to be removed from my body."

Maria had been very aware of life on the inside of her.

"And there were those other women. I thought he loved me? I thought he wanted me to be his woman? I can't believe I'm so stupid!" Maria hated herself for being so weak.

"I can never again go to confession," she continued. "I could never tell this to my priest. And, I'm sure God would never forgive me!"

After several hours of going over and over things in her mind, Maria came to the only conclusion she could see.

She slowly stood up and shivered as the cold, night air penetrated her loosely worn jacket. She started to bundle up, but then thought, *"what's the use?"*

She recklessly moved further out onto the rocky cliff until she was standing on the very edge, looking into the ravine below.

She stood there for a long time, silently sobbing, hoping that maybe someone, or something would intervene and rescue her.

But, there was nothing but darkness and the cold, swirling wind.

After what seemed like an eternity, she closed her eyes, took one last deep breath and gently leaned forward until the force of gravity took over, plunging her body to the bottom of the ravine, 900 feet below!

Chapter Thirty-Four

David Palmer had made up his mind. If Christopher or Pauli found out, he would be branded a traitor. Regardless, he was going to talk with Sheriff Arlan Prichard.

On this wintry day, he was driving into Colorado Springs for supplies. After driving for only five miles, he turned off Highway 24 and headed for the little village of Roper.

Roper was also the county seat, and the location of the Sheriff Prichard's office.

David nervously entered what he had been told was the enemy's camp. A little bluegrass music wafting in the background helped to ease his mind.

"What can I do for you, son," Sheriff Prichard's low, gravelly voice spoke across the desk?

"I don't hardly know where to start," answered David. "Its just that, well, there seems to be some strange things going on up at the Family of God compound."

"Like what?"

"First, it was Momma Elsie. She was old, but in good health. It seems like one day she was walking around the compound, working, talking, laughing, and then, just like that, she was dead!"

"Old people die, son."

"I know, Sheriff, but there's something else. There were rumors that Momma Elsie left Christopher Judah a large sum of money in her will. Right after we began hearing those rumors, she got sick and died."

"Well, son, I'm certain that an autopsy would have shown if it was anything other than a natural death."

"Sheriff, I don't know that there was an autopsy. She was buried right up there on the property."

"Son, I can't go out and just start digging up bodies. I need some sort of evidence other than suspicion."

"But, that's not all, Sheriff. There was this young girl, Maria...."

Sheriff Prichard interrupted him, "you talking about the girl who jumped off the cliff? The evidence said that was a suicide."

"Yeah, I wondered about that," answered David. *"At first, she seemed so happy to be a part of the Family of God; but the more time she spent with Christopher, the less happy she became!"*

Hunters had discovered Maria's body three days after her death. Family of God members thought she had gone home to San Diego.

There was a little investigation, but no proof could be found that Maria's death was anything other than suicide.

Christopher went to great lengths to explain to Sheriff Prichard that Maria was not an emotionally stable person, but that he had tried his best to help her.

Once again, Arlan Prichard was not impressed!

Sheriff Prichard was silent for a few moments before speaking again. *"Son, I'd really like to help you. I must admit, I also have my suspicions about what goes on up at that so-called Promised Land; but what you're talking about here is murder! For such a serious charge, we need to have a little bit more to go on than just suspicion."*

David had a dejected look on his face. He rose from his seat, uttered a disappointed *"thank you,"* and started toward the door.

Ironically, he recalled Christopher's frequent warnings about the inequities of the American system of justice, as compared to the safety and security of their Promised Land.

"Just a minute, son," Sheriff Prichard called him back.

"What you need is one of those investigative reporters. You know, someone who will poke around and dig up some evidence, if there is any."

"Sheriff Prichard, where would I find such a person?"

"Don't know for sure, but you might try the Colorado Springs Herald."

Chapter Thirty-Five

Robert Bernstein sat in the spare office provided for him by the Colorado Springs Herald, pecking away on a word processor.

He was an energetic, young, investigative reporter sent down by a large newspaper in Denver. His boss had told him, *"Rob, go down to Colorado Springs and see what you can find out about this cult group up in the mountains."*

So, David Palmer wasn't alone in his suspicions. Since the story of Maria's leap of death reached the media, there had been quite a lot of unanswered questions about the Family of God.

Rob had started his investigation in the most obvious place; banking records and financial transactions.

He was surprised to learn that Christopher Judah had changed more than one and a half million dollars into gold. *"I think I'm on to something down here,"* he had reported to his boss!

"Excuse me, Mr. Bernstein," one of the secretaries interrupted his thoughts.

"There's a young man here who would like to talk with you. He's a member of that group up in the mountains."

"Is this a stroke of luck, or what," Rob thought to himself as he welcomed David Palmer into his office?

David spilled out his whole story, just as he had done earlier in the day to Sheriff Prichard.

"David," asked Rob Bernstein, *"did you know that Christopher Judah has changed more than one and a half million dollars of Family of God assets into gold?"*

"One and a half million dollars? Are you serious? Are you sure? I didn't know we had a million and a half dollars."

"I'm deadly serious, David. Here, let me show you; I have copies of the financial transactions to prove it."

"To hear Christopher tell it, responded David, *"the Family of God has no money at all. He's always talking about the need to raise more money!"*

"So, David, what's this fellow's real name? Christopher Judah is obviously some made-up spiritual name."

David had to refresh his memory. It had been a long time since anyone had called their spiritual leader anything other than Christopher Judah. *"Uh, Brad, yeah, that's right, Brad Hawkins."*

"Where's he from?"

"Somewhere in Texas, I think."

"And, what's your opinion about this self-proclaimed messiah? You do realize everyone is referring to Christopher Judah as a cult leader?"

David took a few moments to gather his thoughts. *"When I first joined the group, I sincerely believed that Christopher was the messiah, or at least one of the messiahs. There was something supernatural about him. I had watched him progress from a college kid, who led our Bible study, to a powerful, charismatic personality with psychic abilities that drew people to him like a magnet. As for myself, I guess I needed a messiah. I had no purpose or direction for my life."*

David paused once again to organize his thoughts. *"It really hurts me to admit this, but it's looking more and more like Christopher Judah is just a big fake."*

"Worse than that," added Rob, *"it's beginning to look like he's also a murderer and a thief!"*

"*David,*" concluded Rob, "*I think we need to meet again. I would really like to get to the bottom of this mess, but I need your help.*"

"*It won't be easy to continue meeting with you,*" David added. "*I have to be very careful. Christopher has a tight rein on the people up there.*"

That night, David was questioned by Pauli. "*You were gone longer than usual, what's the problem?*"

"*I had a little trouble finding the things we needed,*" David lied. It was going to be difficult keeping secrets from Christopher and Pauli's watchful eyes!

Chapter Thirty-Six

About one month later, Pauli went into Roper on a Sunday afternoon to fill up his pick-up truck with gasoline.

Upon his return, he came bursting into Christopher's room with the Sunday edition of the Colorado Springs Herald. *"Christopher, look at this, there's an article about us in the newspaper."*

Sure enough, right on the front page was an article bearing the headlines:

FAMILY OF GOD CULT
SUSPECTED OF
MURDER AND FRAUD

"Where did they get this information?" Christopher was hurriedly reading through the article. Some of it was absolute fact. Other parts of it, although true, were still in the realm of speculation.

"I don't understand," Christopher said again. *"From where could they have gotten this information? And, who is this reporter, Robert Bernstein?"*

David Palmer had been meeting with Robert Bernstein every time he went into Colorado Springs. He had given Rob every bit of information he knew, both truth and suspicion. Now, here it was, on the front page of the Colorado Springs Herald.

"So where on earth do you think you're going," questioned Cindy Palmer?

"I'm not sure. I just know I'm leaving this place." David continued packing his belongings.

"I don't think you would be welcome at home," Cindy emphasized. *"After all, you withdrew from school and used the refund; which just happened to be your father's money; to come up here in the first place. You certainly don't have a job! All you have to your name is that stupid, old, rundown pick-up!"*

"Listen, Cindy, for more than a month, I've been meeting with an investigative reporter in Colorado Springs.

I've told him everything! Things that I haven't told anyone else but you. It's just a matter of time until all that stuff will be in the newspaper."

"You mean all those wild suspicions about Momma Elsie and Maria?" And, then she added, *"David, my dear boy, you have become a traitor!"*

"That's not all, Cindy. Christopher has more than one and a half million dollars of gold in a safe in his office."

"Oh, come on," Cindy laughed right in his face. *"Now, that's the wildest story of them all!"*

"Cindy, listen to me. I have personally seen copies of the financial transactions. This is not a wild story, it's a fact!"

The wheels in Cindy's mind began to turn. *"A million and a half dollars in gold! Someone was eventually going to enjoy the benefits of those riches."*

She made a decision. She wasn't going with David. For the entire first year, she hated him for bringing her up here. Now, she had gotten used to three good meals a day, and the security of a family. She wasn't going to run off with David again to destination nowhere! Besides, she had a plan!

"Cindy, get packed. I want to get out of here before dark."

"I'm not going."

"What do you mean you're not going? You're my wife!"

"*David, dear, you don't have anywhere to go! You don't have any money, and you don't have a job! If you leave, I'm staying. If you find a job somewhere, you can write me. Maybe I'll come!*"

David wished they had more time to discuss the matter, but even if they did, it was likely to be a waste of time. This was just a reflection of the way their relationship had been going lately.

He shrugged his shoulders in frustration and walked out of their little cubicle in the bunkhouse, his arms loaded with boxes and plastic bags.

Fear swept over him as he saw Christopher and Pauli standing beside his truck.

"*I'm leaving the Family of God,*" David said.

"*Would your leaving have anything to do with this?*" Christopher thrust the newspaper article in his face.

David couldn't answer. He just continued to pack his truck.

"*How could you betray me,*" questioned Christopher? "*You have always been one of my most loyal and trusted members. Do you really believe I'm a murderer and a thief?*"

"*I can't prove it,*" David answered, "*but I suspect that you are.*"

"*Then David, by all means go. We certainly don't want anyone in the Family of God who is not in complete agreement with our purpose.*"

"I was in agreement with your purpose, Christopher, but I'm not in agreement with your methods of fulfilling the purpose!"

As Christopher and Pauli stood back, David laboriously cranked his old pick-up, lurched forward and eased toward the compound exit.

"Christopher, we can't allow him to get away with this," stressed Pauli. *"He knows too much! If he keeps running his mouth, we'll soon have Sheriff Prichard and his deputies crawling all over this place."*

"I agree," added Christopher as he turned and walked back to his office.

Chapter Thirty-Seven

David headed his old pick-up north on Highway 24. He wasn't going back to Colorado Springs; neither was he going to meet again with Robert Bernstein. He had made the decision to completely remove himself from the whole Family of God scene.

He turned west on Highway 82 and headed toward Aspen. *"I think the skiing season is about over,"* he thought to himself. *"Maybe I can still find a temporary job?"*

He checked his road map. *"Looks like about 44 miles. Sure hope I can make it! I probably shouldn't be on this road at this time of the year."*

He knew this highway could be treacherous in the Winter. This particular stretch of Highway 82 passes along side Mt. Elbert, the highest point in Colorado; then through Independence Pass, and across the Continental Divide. Portions of this road are sometimes closed in the Winter.

It was slow going as he maneuvered his old truck through a light, but freshly fallen snow. In some places, there was very little shoulder on the road. Any vehicle sliding off the road faced the possibility of a long drop.

David faintly noticed a pair of distant headlights in his rear view mirror. He was somewhat surprised that another vehicle was on the road. Probably, it was a snow plow, or some other type of rescue vehicle checking the road. That thought temporarily comforted him.

Ten minutes later, he noticed that the vehicle was rapidly gaining on him. *"That person is driving entirely too fast for these wintry conditions,"* he said out loud!

He made the mental decision to look for a place to pull over and let this vehicle pass; but first, there was this long, narrow curve he must negotiate.

A twinge of fear hit the pit of David's stomach. *"That vehicle is really moving fast! Who would be crazy enough to drive like that in these conditions,"* he wondered? *"I'll be glad when that guy is around me!"*

David kept his eyes on the road and his hands steady on the steering wheel, expecting at any moment to see the other vehicle swoosh past him.

Instead, he was jolted by a sudden and tremendous impact that smashed his head against the windshield, shattering the glass, and knocking him unconscious.

Pauli stood on the narrow shoulder of the road, peering into the dark gulch below; his pick-up noisily idling in the background.

He had watched as David's truck skidded off the highway and slowly began to slide down the steep incline.

He had watched as it picked up speed and began to tumble end over end, finally bouncing off a large boulder and coming to rest upside down about 600 feet below.

Now, he was peering into the darkness, looking and listening for any signs of life. There was nothing but an occasional whistling of the wind.

As Pauli walked back to his truck, he chuckled to himself. There was no noticeable damage. He had one of those thick wooden bumpers mounted on the front.

Snow plows discovered David's truck the next day. If the crash didn't kill him, he would have frozen to death during the night.

The news media made a special effort to remind the public that they should not be traveling on this stretch of highway at this time of the year, especially at night!

Everyone just assumed that David lost control of his vehicle due to the slippery conditions.

That is, everyone except Robert Bernstein!

Chapter Thirty-Eight

Several days later, Christopher walked into his office and found Pauli propped up with his feet on the desk.

"Morning Chris," he said.

"What did you call me," Christopher was taken aback?

"Chris, you know, it's the short version of Christopher."

"Don't ever call me by that name again. My name is Christopher Judah, and I am the God ordained, spiritual leader of the Family of God!"

"You're also potentially in a great deal of trouble," reported Pauli.

"*And so are you,*" added Christopher. "*Exactly what's going on here? Are you also becoming disloyal?*"

"*Absolutely not, my friend. Although I'm not too sure about this God appointed thing anymore; I am nonetheless committed to you and to your cause.*"

"*Well then, what's this all about?*"

"*Christopher, my friend, I just want to make sure that you are also loyal to me. I've gone way out on a limb for you, and I want to be sure that we're in this thing together. I need some assurance that we will continue to be a team.*"

"*Pauli, you have my word on it. I need you to help me run this operation. We are a team! And, as far as David Palmer's unfortunate demise is concerned, he got what was coming to him. We can't allow zealous fools to destroy what we're building.*"

Later that day, Cindy Palmer walked right past Naomi and walked into Christopher's office, unannounced and without an appointment.

"*You had him killed, didn't you?*"

Christopher quickly walked over and closed the door. "*Cindy, please, calm down. Here, sit down and let's talk.*"

"*Listen, Christopher, I know you had him killed, and probably the others also.*"

"*Others? What others?*"

"Momma Elsie and Maria."

"Cindy, you must be misinformed. You don't know what you're saying...."

She interrupted him, *"I know about the gold too!"*

Christopher's countenance dramatically changed, as if some closely guarded secret in his life had been uncovered. *"So, what's this, Cindy, a blackmail scheme?"*

"I want to make a deal with you, Christopher."

"What kind of deal?"

"First of all," she said, *" I don't care about David. He was a loser anyway. I'm glad he's gone!"*

Cindy moved closer to Christopher, sat on the edge of his desk and looked temptingly into his eyes. *"What I want, Christopher, is to be your woman. I already know about Naomi and Maria, but I can take better care of you than either of them."*

"You must be joking," answered Christopher. *"Surely that's not all you want? You must want some of my gold too?"*

"What I want, Christopher, is to enjoy the benefits of the gold!"

The truth was, Christopher had wanted Cindy for a long time; and she had noticed him watching her. He was actually trying to figure out a way to take her away from David when Maria came along, providing him with a temporary reprieve from lusting for Cindy.

"*Cindy,*" he smiled, "*you have a deal!*"

On that same day, she moved into the main house, something not even Maria or Naomi had been allowed to do.

Also, on that same day, Naomi vowed in her heart that somehow, she would get even with Christopher!

So, Christopher gained a woman that day; and he solidified his alliance with Pauli, but he also lost something.

Previous to this time, the entire Family of God was totally devoted to him. They looked upon him with awe and reverence.

Now, his frailty had been exposed. The results being that he had allowed two people to penetrate his cloak of deception, and get closer to him than he ever intended.

But, make no mistake about it, he was still solidly in charge. His superior intellect and ability to control situations made him indispensable!

Chapter Thirty-Nine

In the midst of these current problems, Christopher had to make a trip back to Cartersville.

He received word that Belinda Sue had died of lung cancer at the young age of 43.

Actually, he had been receiving phone calls from Uncle Frank and Aunt Pearl for the past several months, informing him that his mom was dying, and emphasizing that she was asking to see him before she died.

Christopher was unmoved, having long since severed his family ties. The reason he was going home now was because there was mention of a will left by Belinda Sue.

This time when he arrived in Cartersville, there was no heroes welcome. There were no free meals, no free haircuts, and no invitations to speak to school children.

In fact, almost no one spoke to him at all. People he had grown up with and gone to school with just curiously stared at him.

He was now an infamous cult leader; and maybe a murderer and thief if the newspaper articles were true. The town's people just didn't know how to approach him, or what they would say if they did!

Even the *"politically correct"* Mayor Raeford Smiley couldn't think of anything appropriate to say. Christopher eased the situation by ignoring him.

Of course, there was the usual gossip down at the beauty parlor. *"Well, I just can't imagine what went wrong with Bradley!" "That boy had a lot of potential, you know!" "His mom cried a million tears over him!"*

There was a distinct difference in the way Christopher viewed the town's folks of Cartersville, as compared to the way they viewed him.

Christopher still looked upon the Cartersville people as small-minded and limited in their scope of experience and understanding; while viewing himself as the successful founder and leader of a spiritually enlightened community; not to mention the fact that he had more than one and a half million dollars of gold.

On the other hand, the good citizens of Cartersville saw Bradley as someone who was offered a great opportunity to better himself despite his unfortunate beginnings.

What Bradley had done instead; in light of their higher standards of morality and family values; had placed him, in their eyes, in the category of a miserable failure!

Almost the entire town turned out for the funeral. It wasn't that they cared about Belinda Sue. Most of them came to watch Christopher. Maybe they thought he would perform some religious rite.

The local pastor was clearly intimidated by Christopher's presence, and nervously hurried through the service.

Among the crowd, Christopher recognized Low Boy's profile as he shuffled about, hiding behind people, trying to make himself as inconspicuous as possible.

His business dealings with Uncle Frank and Aunt Pearl were curt and quite to the point.

They did manage to muster up a word or two of admonishment. *"Bradley, your mother really needed you these past few months,"* said Uncle Frank. *"I feel that you let her down in her time of greatest need." "Every day she asked about you,"* added Aunt Pearl. *"She believed you would come."*

His response was quick and cold. *"My mom died because she polluted herself with at least three packs of cigarettes everyday!"*

Christopher didn't bother to even greet Richard or Timothy.

Glenda was sternly instructed by Aunt Pearl not to get involved with, nor to even talk to Bradley.

Belinda Sue's estate wasn't much to talk about. A few acres of land, Grandma Nell's dilapidated house, and a rusty, old car that needed a lot of maintenance and repair. Some additional household items were sold at an auction.

Uncle Frank and Aunt Pearl reluctantly offered Christopher $75,000.00 for the land and the house; desiring to have something to give their kids.

Christopher quickly accepted the offer, finished up his business, and headed back to Colorado; determined in his heart that he would never again return to this dying, little town.

Chapter Forty

Back in Colorado, Christopher doubled his efforts in instructing the Family of God and in developing the Promised Land.

Taking advantage of Robert Bernstein's accusations, he continued to improperly use the scriptures to gain an advantage, *"Yes,"* he would say, *"all who desire to live godly will suffer persecution."* He assured the Family of God that this campaign of hurtful lies was the work of the enemy.

He continued to prophesy an imminent financial collapse upon the United States; while at the same time, emphasizing the stability, security and self-sufficiency of their own environment.

He continued to emphasize the importance of their deliverance from the corruption, pollution, violence and injustice of the outside world; and to assure the people that here in their Promised Land, they were not only safe from the outside world, but more importantly, they were preparing themselves for their eternal home.

In his polished and flattering style, he would look intently at the people, and say, *"I know of no other place in the United States where someone can discover God. As we approach our two year anniversary here in the Promised Land, I am reminded of the words of the Psalmist David: 'Surely, goodness and mercy shall follow me all the days of my life; and I will dwell in the house of the Lord forever.'"*

As warm, Spring days graced the compound, their industries began to flourish. In addition to PROMISED LAND NATURAL AND ORGANIC FOODS, they began to market: PROMISED LAND CRYSTAL CLEAR MOUNTAIN WATER, and PROMISED LAND WHOLE GRAIN BREADS.

These products proved to be very popular among the health food adherents in the surrounding communities.

Consequently, they built a small, walk-in store near the entrance of the compound so passers-by could purchase their products.

The Family of God was making great strides toward becoming self-sufficient and self-supporting. Windmills now dotted the landscape of the property. Beef and dairy cattle roamed their pastures. Roosters crowing and chickens squawking accompanied every morning.

Arguably, Christopher Judah had done an excellent job in managing close to 400 people, successfully perpetrating a strong work ethic, creating self-sufficiency and eliminating idleness from their lives.

However, the lies, murder and fraud that somehow seemed justifiably necessary to maintain his shroud of deception were beginning to cause a strain in their seemingly impregnable existence.

Robert Bernstein had become a major problem. He was determined to prove that Christopher was involved in David Palmer's death, and if possible, Momma Elsie and Maria Mendoza's death as well.

He began to hang around Roper, trying to talk to any members of the Family of God that came into the little village.

His efforts weren't all that easy. It was infrequent these days that members of the Family came into Roper. They didn't have any money; and transportation was limited and regulated!

All current profits from their industries were turned into the office at the end of each day and became Family of God assets.

There was a time when members of the Family came into Roper almost on a daily basis. Of course, in the early days, many of them had cars. They would come to make phone calls, buy newspapers or just to buy hamburgers.

But, these days, their contact with the outside world was becoming less and less. Some of them had even become fearful of leaving the compound. They had literally given their all to Christopher Judah.

Consequently, Rob Bernstein's efforts were largely unrewarded. Most of those he did talk to were closed-mouthed and fiercely loyal to Christopher and the Family of God.

Nevertheless, his articles continued to appear in the Colorado Springs Herald. Any little discontentment or note of discord he could detect from Family of God members would be worked into a story.

This was a source of great irritation and anger to Christopher. He was determined that somehow he would eventually get even with this nosy reporter.

Chapter Forty-One

Horace *"Buck"* Buchanan tightened his seat belt as the McDonnell Douglas Super 80 Jetliner made one final banking turn on its approach into Denver's international airport.

Buck didn't exactly look like an FBI agent. Old rumpled suit, shirt tail half out, hair somewhere between uncombed and half combed and a tacky tie worn loosely around his neck.

But, this was one man that should not be underestimated. He had an experienced understanding of the criminal mind, a keen sense of intuition and a sharp eye for detail.

After landing, he hurried through the deplaning area out into the main terminal, and quickly lit up a cigarette.

As he temporarily satisfied his habit, he looked disgustingly at the cigarette. *"I wish I could rid my life of this filthy plague,"* he thought as he continued to puff away.

There was a time when these things had no control over him. He fondly remembered his days at the FBI Academy in Quantico, Virginia. He was physically fit, disciplined and in control of his life.

However, most of his career as an FBI agent had consisted of long hours and a desk at the Washington, D.C. headquarters stacked high with overdue paperwork.

At the end of a typical work day, he would often be amazed as he observed his surroundings. There on his desk was a large ashtray, overflowing with a mountain of smelly cigarette butts and ashes. On his right was a government issue trash can full of styrofoam cups. He had literally existed that day on cigarettes and coffee!

Although he had to beg his superior to get this field assignment, he was really glad to finally get out of the office. He was looking forward to the clean, crisp, mountain air.

Maybe the motel would have a fitness center; or maybe he could start a jogging program. Well, at first, it would have to be a walking program; but maybe, just maybe he could get himself back into better shape.

On the short commuter flight down to Colorado Springs, he reviewed the rather thin file the FBI had accumulated on Christopher Judah and the Family of God.

"There's sure not much to go on here," he thought to himself. *"This guy has kept a low profile. He's done a pretty good job of maintaining secrecy in his outfit."*

The FBI wouldn't even be involved except that Maria Mendoza's parents caused quite a stir after her death. They insisted that she had been kidnapped by the Family of God.

Rob Bernstein had been sending them copies of his newspaper articles from the Colorado Springs Herald; and they had subsequently hired a private investigator who tried, unsuccessfully, to build a case against the Family of God.

In addition, because of Christopher's prophetic letters to certain elected government officials, the FBI had decided to open and maintain a file on the Family of God to determine whether they might prove to be a risk to national security.

Later that afternoon, Buck sat in Sheriff Arlan Prichard's office puffing away on his usual cigarette and pouring down a cup of strong, black coffee. *"Oh well,"* he thought, *"maybe I'll get going on my fitness program tomorrow!"*

"This guy's got all the bases covered," explained Sheriff Prichard. "There's a good possibility he's responsible for three deaths, but we don't have any proof. I've been waiting for him to slip up, but so far, he's been pretty slick!"

"I see here that you classified Maria Mendoza's death as a suicide?" Buck was reviewing Sheriff Prichard's files and asking questions.

"Yeah, and to tell you the truth, suicide is a very real possibility. The folks who live up there in the Promised Land aren't exactly the most stable and well adjusted citizens of our community.

As for her parent's claim that she was kidnapped, I would say that's highly unlikely. The best we can determine, she ran off with some rodeo star in San Diego. She apparently was rescued by the Family of God after he dumped her."

"I also see that David Palmer's death was officially classified as an accident," Buck continued.

"Don't have any evidence otherwise," said Sheriff Prichard. "Apparently, he was a victim of hazardous driving conditions."

"What about this lady, Momma Elsie? Who was she?"

"Just one of the senior citizens up at the Promised Land. According to the coroner's report, she just died of old age."

"Was there an autopsy?"

"Not that I know of. I guess at the time, there didn't seem to be any need for one.

But I will tell you one thing, that young man, David Palmer was totally convinced that Momma Elsie died under mysterious circumstances. Said it had something to do with her will. Apparently, she left this guy, Christopher Judah quite a lot of money."

"How do you know that?"

"Well, since I didn't have any real evidence on Christopher Judah, I recommended to David Palmer that he find an investigative reporter. You know, someone who would snoop around and dig up some trash. He found a good one!"

Sheriff Prichard stood up, walked over to a shelf and returned with a stack of newspapers.

"This guy, Bernstein has been printing stories about Christopher Judah and the Family of God about twice a week. Don't know how much is truth or fiction, but it makes for interesting reading."

Buck scribbled a note in his pocket calendar to track down Robert Bernstein first thing tomorrow morning.

"Thanks Sheriff Prichard," he concluded, *"I really appreciate all your help. I'm looking forward to working with you in the coming days."*

"I'm glad I could be of service, Agent Buchanan. Don't hesitate to ask if I can be of further assistance."

"Sheriff Prichard," Buck interjected, "my first name is Horace, but everyone calls me Buck. I would appreciate it if you would do the same."

"That goes the same for me, Buck. You can call me Arlan."

Chapter Forty-Two

The next morning, Buck Buchanan and Robert Bernstein were enjoying scrambled eggs with homemade biscuits and gravy at a country style diner just up the street from the Colorado Springs Herald.

"I'll tell you what, Buck. I believe Brad Hawkins, alias Christopher Judah is responsible for all three deaths; and I think David Palmer, in particular, was killed to keep him from talking about the other two.

Unfortunately, I don't yet have any hard evidence, but my gut feeling tells me he's totally responsible. Furthermore, I intend to find the evidence and prove him guilty."

"Well, it looks like you're off to a good start, Robert. I recommend that we work together on this matter, and not allow any competition between us. Hopefully, we can get this guy, Christopher Judah behind bars before he causes another David Koresh or Jim Jones incident."

"Agreed, and you can call me Rob. By the way, Buck, where are you staying?"

"The cheapest motel I could find."

"Listen Buck, I despise motel living; and I can tolerate only so much restaurant food. So, I rented a mountain cabin about 20 miles out of Colorado Springs. There's plenty of room there, and it would put you closer to the Promised Land compound, and closer to Sheriff Prichard's office. Why not move in with me?"

"Rob, you have yourself a deal."

Later that night, Buck was stretched out in a recliner, watching the Colorado Rockies on television. Unfortunately, they happened to be playing the Atlanta Braves. The play-by-play announcer promised that in time, the Rockies would be right up there, competing for the pennant. As the game crept into the ninth inning, Buck drifted off to sleep.

It was about 11:00 PM when Rob Bernstein finally left the office. There was still a hustle and bustle about the office as the staff prepared the morning edition of the Herald.

As he pulled his Corvette out of the parking lot, Rob didn't notice the big, black pick-up that pulled in behind him.

It was a beautiful night, and a fantastic drive as he roared up Highway 24 with the cool breeze flowing in the sun roof.

He was deep in thought and never even noticed the occasional flickering of distant headlights in his rear view mirror.

As he turned onto the narrow mountain road that led to the cabin, he was surprised to see a vehicle turn and follow him.

"Must be someone from the office," he reasoned, trying to remember if he forgot to add, delete or correct something in his latest article. *"Maybe it's that nice looking, young lady from the editing section,"* he wished, smiling to himself.

He pulled into the driveway, got out of his car and started walking back toward the road just as the big, black pick-up pulled up.

"Good evening," he said, trying to see who was in the vehicle.

His stroll toward the other vehicle was abruptly interrupted by the piercing of three rapidly fired bullets tearing into his chest!

As Rob collapsed on the concrete driveway, bleeding and gasping for breath, Pauli carefully looked around to see if there was anyone else in the vicinity.

Then, he casually got out of his truck, walked over to Rob and pumped three more bullets into his dying body.

Buck was suddenly awakened by the screeching of tires. He had not heard the shots which were muffled by a silencer.

He sleepily walked to the front door, expecting to chastise Rob for the way he drove his sports car. Instead, what he saw was Rob's lifeless body lying in a pool of blood.

In the distance, he could make out a dark colored, pick-up truck speeding down the narrow mountain road and turning west on Highway 24. Unfortunately, it was too dark to clearly recognize the make, year or actual color of the truck.

"Arlan, wake up! This is Buck. Listen, Rob Bernstein is lying out here in the driveway, dead! He's been shot five, maybe six times. How soon can you get together a swat team and a search warrant? We've got to get up to the Promised Land as quickly as possible!"

"I'll get to work on it. It will probably take a couple of hours, so why don't you head this way?"

"I'm on my way, Arlan!"

Chapter Forty-Three

Christopher nervously paced the floor of his office, occasionally looking at Cindy, and then looking at his watch. It was past 1:00 AM. Pauli should be back by now.

Earlier that night, they had conducted a secret meeting. He was anxiously recalling the events of that meeting.

"If we don't do something about this guy, Bernstein," Christopher was explaining, *"our whole world is going to come tumbling down."*

"What can we do," asked Cindy? *"This is a free country, and that includes freedom of the press."*

Pauli sat quietly by, listening to their conversation. Finally, he spoke. *"I can take care of the matter."*

"How," they asked simultaneously?

Pauli left the room, and returned a few minutes later with something wrapped in a towel. As he carefully unfolded the towel, Christopher recognized a 9MM pistol, two clips, a box of ammunition and a silencer.

"I know you told me not to buy a gun," Pauli explained, *"but I thought we might need one. This one is unregistered and the serial number has been filed off."*

Cindy was noticeably upset. *"Hey, wait a minute, you guys; I don't want anything to do with this type of thing!"*

"Whether you like it or not, you're already involved," Pauli said. *"And Cindy, don't forget, if the Family of God falls, the gold will be gone too!"*

"Can't we just sue him or something," she asked?

Christopher was silent for a while, not responding to Cindy's last question. Then, taking a deep breath, he asked, *"Pauli, can you accomplish such a task without leaving any evidence that could point to us?"*

"You know that I can," answered Pauli.

Christopher's thoughts were interrupted by the sound of Pauli's truck coming up the ranch road from Highway 24.

He and Cindy quietly, but anxiously waited in the office.

Pauli hurriedly walked in, noticeably nervous and still breathing rapidly.

"Well?"

"It's done," answered Pauli. *"The only thing left undone is to discard this gun. I'm going to drive up to the edge of our property and find a deep place in the stream."*

As Pauli was leaving, he was suddenly called back by Christopher. *"Wait, Pauli, don't discard the gun just yet. There is still one thing left undone!"*

"Now the Spirit expressly says that in latter times some will depart from the faith, giving heed to deceiving spirits and doctrines of demons.... HAVING THEIR OWN CONSCIENCE SEARED WITH A HOT IRON."

> The Apostle Paul
> First Epistle to Timothy
> From Chapter 4, verses 1 & 2

Chapter Forty-Four

At 5:00 in the morning, Sheriff Arlan Prichard, Buck Buchanan and 15 deputies noisily descended on the Promised Land.

Ten law enforcement vehicles quickly formed a perimeter around the main house, lights flashing, sirens blaring.

Within seconds, they were crouched behind their vehicles, armed with shotguns and semiautomatic assault rifles.

Buck addressed Christopher through a megaphone, *"Christopher Judah, this is FBI Agent Buck Buchanan. We have your house surrounded. Come out slowly with your hands in the air."*

Christopher and Cindy emerged from the house, appearing sleepy. Actually, they hadn't slept all night.

"*Please don't shoot,*" Christopher called out! "*Please don't harm anyone! We are a peace loving community.*"

He then recognized Sheriff Prichard. With great concern in his voice, he asked, "*Sheriff Prichard, whatever is the meaning of this illegal intrusion?*"

"*Son, this is Agent Buck Buchanan from the Federal Bureau of Investigation; and this is not an illegal intrusion. We have a warrant to search this property.*"

"*A search warrant, Sheriff. May I inquire as to what you hope to find?*"

Christopher's last question was ignored; and he was left holding the warrant while deputies began a deliberate search of the main house.

By this time, members of the Family of God had filed out of their living quarters and were standing around the main house with quizzical looks on their faces.

Some of them raised their voices in protest, "*Why are you persecuting us?*" "*We have harmed no one!*" "*Please go away and leave us alone!*"

Christopher quieted the people and then addressed them. "*Brothers and sisters, I don't know what this is all about, but I can assure you that it's all a big mistake. Go back to your living quarters and prepare for *a normal day. And, remember, God is on our side!"*

"I want to see all the vehicles owned by this organization," Buck interrupted Christopher's speech.

"Yes sir," answered Christopher. *"We are more than happy to cooperate...."*

"Save the sweet talk, just show me the vehicles."

Christopher showed him the off-road, four wheel drive vehicle, and the motorcycle which he personally owned; and two old vans which they used to transport Family of God members.

"Where's the big, dark colored, pick-up truck," asked Buck?

"Pick-up?" Christopher at first had a puzzled look on his face, but then replied, *"Actually, yes, one of our members does own a pick-up, but he's away on business for a few days."*

After several hours, the deputies, one by one emerged from the house, shaking their heads in a negative manner.

"We'll also have a look in your safe," Buck demanded.

Christopher reluctantly led Buck and Sheriff Prichard into his office and opened the safe.

Buck and Arlan just stood there for a few moments, appearing stunned. Sheriff Prichard finally spoke up, *"whatever are you going to do with all this gold?"*

"Sheriff Prichard, I'm surprised that you don't recognize the signs of the times," answered Christopher. *"Don't you realize that we are facing an imminent financial collapse of our nation's monetary systems? We're living on borrowed time in a dying world!"*

"No, son, I didn't realize that!"

"When that financial collapse occurs" Christopher continued, *"we here in the Promised Land will not be affected."*

"Hawkins," Buck interrupted him again, *"we didn't find what we were looking for this morning, but I can promise you that we'll be back. I'm convinced that you're responsible for the deaths of four people, and I intend to prove it."*

As Buck was walking out of the house, he glanced in Cindy's direction, not knowing who she was. Her eyes temporarily met his, and she quickly turned away, leaving the impression that she knew something.

As he reached the porch, he stopped, turned back and spoke again to Christopher, *"by the way, Hawkins, don't entertain any thoughts about gunning down an FBI agent like you disposed of Robert Bernstein. I can assure you that I'll be ready and waiting!"*

"Agent Buchanan, my name is Christopher Judah, and I am the spiritual leader of the Family of God. And, what's this about someone named Bernstein? Was someone killed recently?"

Buck gave him a disgusted look, and then responded, *"your legal name is Bradley Eugene Hawkins and you're from Cartersville, Texas. That's the name I'll be calling you by. I'm not fooled by your spiritual pretension."*

As they departed, Christopher had to fire one last verbal shot, *"Agent Buchanan, I couldn't possibly imagine any reason why you would ever again visit this ranch!"*

"Oh, I'll be back, Hawkins. You can count on it!"

Chapter Forty-Five

Low Boy moved slowly around the interior of his restaurant, checking the doors, making sure they were all locked.

Cowboy Clyde Hankins and the El Paso Wranglers were packing up the last of their musical instruments and sound equipment after a rip-roaring Country and Western hoedown.

There were still a few slurred conversations going on in the parking lot regarding designated drivers, as if it made a difference.

The last two girls walked out, still giggling about an encounter they had earlier in the evening with an out-of-town cowboy.

Low Boy finally turned out the lights and waited by the front door for the bartender, who handed him a bulging bank bag containing the night's receipts.

He locked the front door and glanced at his watch. 2:30 AM.

The parking lot was silent now, even though it was full of eighteen wheelers. The drivers were all tucked away in their cabs, or in one of Low Boy's cheap motel rooms.

Low Boy waddled across the parking lot toward his gold, Cadillac Eldorado. He was now 60 years old; and had gained quite a lot of weight through the years.

As he fumbled around in his pockets, breathing heavily, looking for his keys; he was completely unaware of the big, black pick-up parked nearby. Just another truck which nightly filled his parking lot.

The stillness of the warm, night air was barely disturbed by the muffled sound of three quick *"thuds."*

Low Boy lay crumpled in the parking lot, the upper half of his body lying against the front wheel of his Cadillac.

Pauli drove slowly over to Low Boy's body. He watched for a few moments to see if he was dead. Just to make sure, he fired three more shots into his body.

Across the parking lot, Pauli could see the bartender running toward him. He jammed his foot against the gas petal, swerving and screeching his tires as he sped away.

Early the next morning, just before daylight, Pauli stopped his truck on a bridge crossing the Purgatoire River, just inside the Colorado border.

He waited several minutes until the few vehicles on the road that time of morning were out of sight. He got out of his truck, carrying a heavy looking object.

He hesitated for a few more moments, looking in both directions, making sure there was no oncoming traffic.

Then, he heaved the object as far over the side as he could throw it. To be more specific, the object was a large, heavy brick to which was attached a tightly wrapped package containing a 9MM pistol, two ammunition clips, a silencer and the remaining rounds from one box of ammunition.

He watched, waited and listened until he heard a loud splash.

The evidence Buck Buchanan needed was now at the bottom of the river, soon to be buried in mud!

Later that same day, an exhausted Pauli pulled his pick-up into the Promised Land compound.

Christopher met him in the parking lot with the news. *"We had visitors yesterday morning. Sheriff Prichard, an FBI agent called Buck and a whole bunch of deputies searching the main house.*

"Even more significant," he continued, *"was their acute interest in finding a big, dark colored, pick-up truck! Someone must have seen you!"*

Pauli pulled his tired body back into his truck, remembering that the bartender had also seen the pick-up. *"Not to worry,"* he said, *"I'll take care of the matter."*

He drove for about 15 minutes to the southern most edge of the ranch, where he and Christopher had accidentally discovered an old mine shaft.

He drove about 30 feet into the shaft, stopped and got out. *"Well, old boy,"* he said, patting the front fender, *"you've been good one. Who knows, maybe we'll see one another again, and maybe we won't!"*

After hiking for about an hour, he made it back to the compound, fell into bed and tried to get some sleep.

Sleep didn't come quickly. There was something very strong on his mind that he needed to discuss with Christopher as soon as possible.

Chapter Forty-Six

Buck moved out of the mountain cabin, and moved into a Bed and Breakfast style guest house in Roper. He wanted to be as close as possible to the Promised Land compound.

He set up a mini-headquarters in one of Sheriff Prichard's spare offices, and began a thorough, step-by-step investigation of all possible criminal activities to which Christopher Judah could be linked.

Unfortunately, after several days of exploring every possible lead he could think of, he ended up with the same dead end as Rob Bernstein; suspicion, but no proof.

He could find no evidence of kidnapping in Maria Mendoza's arrival and stay at the Promised Land. The investigation of her death left no other conclusion but suicide.

David Palmer's truck was thoroughly examined. The report revealed nothing except a probable accident.

There was not one shred of evidence to link Christopher to Rob Bernstein's murder. The forensic report revealed that the murder weapon was a 9MM pistol, but where was the pistol?

Buck was grasping for straws, *"maybe the Family of God is secretly growing marijuana up there in the Promised Land and selling it to the citizens of Roper?"*

"Nope," replied Sheriff Prichard. *"I've already explored that avenue. The Family of God has this thing about a pure body and a pure mind. They're always talking about the dangers of pollution. And, it's not just an environmental thing. It has something to do with their obtaining of eternal life."*

"Then, I suppose there's no reason to look into the possibility that they're making illegal moonshine," laughed Buck?

The next morning, Buck came up with a new idea. *"Arlan, let's drive down to Cartersville, and talk to the town's people. Let's talk to Hawkins' relatives, and to his former friends, if he had any."*

On the drive to Cartersville, they crossed over the same bridge where Pauli, just a few days earlier, had disposed of the pistol they so desperately needed as evidence.

The good citizens of Cartersville were interesting, but not very helpful. What Buck needed was a start, just any small piece of evidence that he could build upon.

As a courtesy, they checked in with the local police chief, Roscoe *"Tiny"* Peoples.

Chief Peoples earned his nickname due to the 300 pounds he packed onto his six foot, six inch frame.

Until recently, there wasn't much of a need for any such thing as a criminal investigation in this little town where everybody was related, or knew one another; and also knew one another's business.

Tiny mostly hung around Low Boy's and broke up an occasional fight between out-of-towners or drunks.

He took Sheriff Prichard and Buck on the grand tour of the town.

"That boy was wild," explained Uncle Frank. *"He was disrespectful, spoiled and undisciplined; and I'm sorry to say, it was mostly due to my sister's poor parenting."*

"He deeply hurt his mom," added Aunt Pearl.

His cousins, Richard, Tim and Glenda added their comments. *"He was a spoiled brat." "He always had to be in control." "If he didn't get his way, he would start a fight."*

"That boy had tremendous potential," emphasized the high school principal. "He could have been a doctor, lawyer, congressman, maybe even president!"

"We figured he might become famous some day," commented Mayor Smiley. "We sort of thought he might put Cartersville on the map."

"He has," replied Buck!

"When that boy first left here, he was the pride of Cartersville." They were listening to some of the men down at the barber shop. "Yeah, but then he went off the deep end, got weird!"

They decided not to go to the beauty parlor.

Just as they were about ready to head back to Colorado, Tiny Peoples just casually mentioned, "yeah, we had a murder here a few days ago. We figure it was the work of the mob."

"Who was killed," asked Buck?

"Oh, a fellow everyone called Low Boy. He owned a truck stop just outside of town. Funny, even though he was shot six times, nobody heard any shots. Those mob hit men use silencers, you know."

Tiny continued to ramble on, "Low Boy was one of our most generous citizens. He built the playground we have here in town."

"Chief Peoples," interrupted Buck, "did anybody see or hear anything? Was there any evidence at all?"

"Well, the bartender saw this big, dark colored pick-up speeding away from the parking lot. You know, one of those trucks with oversized tires and a big front bumper. But, it was too dark for him to get the make or license number."

Buck and Sheriff Prichard looked at each other, as if a light bulb had been turned on in the darkness.

"Chief, did Bradley Hawkins have any connection to this fellow, Low Boy?"

"Well, come to think of it, yes he did. His mom, Belinda Sue Hawkins used to be a waitress at Low Boy's restaurant; but that was many years ago.

"So, did Bradley's mom have some kind of quarrel or disagreement with Low Boy," questioned Buck?

"Well, not that I know of."

Then, another light bulb clicked on in Buck's mind. *"Chief Peoples; the waitresses at Low Boy's; are they engaged in any other activities besides waiting on tables?"*

"Well, there have been some rumors...."

Buck interrupted him again, *"who was Bradley Hawkins' father?"*

"Well, come to think of it," Tiny was scratching his head, *"nobody ever knew who Bradley's father was?"*

The pieces of the puzzle were now beginning to come together. Bradley Hawkins had been conceived in one of Low Boy's motel rooms.

Now, through some strange, twisted sense of responsibility; maybe because he was deprived of having a father; Christopher had gained revenge on the man who was indirectly responsible for his birth.

The trouble was, they had no proof!

As they were driving back to Colorado, Buck was going over what they had learned in Cartersville. *"Well, we now know that Hawkins doesn't personally do the killing. He has his own hit man, although we don't know who he is! But, there's no doubt that Hawkins is the one giving the orders!"*

Suddenly, Buck abruptly changed the subject, *"Arlan, I need you to do something for me."*

"Name it."

"It just occurred to me that we don't have any fingerprints or even a photograph of this guy, Hawkins. I need you to bring him in, keep him overnight in jail, run him through the routine. He might try to slip away from us."

"I need something to charge him with."

"Well, think up something. Disturbing the peace, selling illegal water, walking on the grass, anything!"

"O.K. Buck, you got it."

Chapter Forty-Seven

Meanwhile, another secret meeting had been called at the Promised Land, this time at Pauli's request. He, Cindy and Christopher were huddled in the office.

"Christopher," Pauli asked, *"what do you call it when your plans don't work out, and maybe you have to go to plan B?"*

"You mean contingency plans," Christopher answered?

"Yeah, whatever. Anyway, I think we need to develop such a plan"

"Exactly what type of plan are you talking about," asked Christopher?

"A plan of escape," emphasized Pauli!

Christopher seemed irritated, as if he didn't want to hear this, but finally replied, *"O.K., I'm listening."*

"There's an island in the Caribbean," Pauli began to explain. *"A small island by the name of Cay San Pueblo. The interesting thing is, the government there doesn't have an agreement with the United States to send back criminals."*

"You mean an extradition agreement," added Christopher.

"Yeah, whatever. Anyway, if you're living there, even if you're wanted for a crime in the United States, the Cay San Pueblo government is not obligated to send you back. With a little money placed into the hands of the right island officials, we could insure that they would never send us back!"

"Pauli, I don't know anything about the Caribbean. How would we get there?"

"By boat!"

"You mean on a cruise ship or something?"

"No, I mean on our own luxury yacht."

"And who do you think would captain this yacht?"

"I would, Christopher! You see, before I came out to San Francisco, I spent my entire life helping my father and uncle pilot tug boats around the Great Lakes. I know how to read charts, I understand navigation.

And, we could even live on a boat until we found something more permanent."

"Sounds good to me," Cindy added her two cents.

"Pauli," Christopher responded, *"I'm very reluctant to leave here. I've worked so hard to build the Promised Land; and who would take care of the Family of God?"*

"Christopher, if they somehow pin a murder on us, there won't be no Promised Land, and there won't be no more Family of God either!

Besides, when we got settled, we could send for the Family of God. We could start over and build a new Promised Land in our own little island paradise. It beats going to prison!"

"Exactly where is this island?"

"Oh, it's about 90 miles southeast of Jamaica. It's a nice little island. I've been there several times with my father."

Christopher looked somewhat dejected. *"Well, I suppose it's all right for you to look into the matter; but really now, there's no evidence linking us to anyone's death. In time, I'm sure things will settle down and return back to normal."*

Suddenly, their meeting was interrupted by Sheriff Prichard and one of his deputies arriving at the main house.

One overly zealous, young member of the Family of God jumped in front of him as he mounted the steps. *"Sheriff, I protest this intrusion, and your continued persecution of the Family of God!"*

Sheriff Prichard hesitated just briefly. *"Son, I'm going to give you about one second to get out of my way before I throw you off this porch."*

The young man quickly retreated.

"Christopher Judah," barked Sheriff Prichard. *"I'm placing you under arrest for violating county business ordinances. You'll have to come with us. Deputy, read him his rights."*

"You can't be serious, Sheriff. We have complied with every regulation!"

"Now, son, don't give us any trouble. Just come along peacefully, and if we can get this matter straightened out, you'll be back up here in no time."

The next morning, Christopher was returned to the Promised Land.

"It was all a trumped-up charge," he reported. *"The only reason I was arrested was to get my photograph and fingerprints. Under any other circumstances, I would sue them for false arrest."*

"Christopher," Pauli explained, *"I took the liberty of booking flights to Miami. It's time to go shopping for a boat!"*

"I guess you're right," Christopher reluctantly replied. *"Please gather the Family of God in the assembly hall. I'll inform them that we must be away for several days, and encourage them to keep the faith!"*

Chapter Forty-Eight

It was 9:00 AM, several mornings later. Christopher, Pauli and Cindy sat in one of the ritzy offices of Sea Worthy, Inc., builders of luxury yachts.

"Top O the morning to you, gentlemen, and to you young lady," a very prim and proper middle aged man addressed them as he entered the office. *"I'm Nigil Winthrop, your representative."*

Nigil Charles Thomas-Winthrop was originally from England. His parents had moved to Jamaica in his teenage years, and had purchased large quantities of land on the island.

Later, his family had become wealthy from the bauxite mining industry.

When Jamaica won its independence from Great Britain in 1962, Nigil had moved to Miami; and subsequently started a luxury boat building business.

"*Good morning to you, Mr. Winthrop. I'm Brad Hawkins, this is Paul Wolenski, and you may call this young lady, Cindy.*"

"*And, how may I be of assistance to you this morning,*" he asked? As they were talking, a young lady served English breakfast tea, scones and marmalade.

"*Mr. Winthrop, we're in the market for an ocean going yacht,*" Christopher replied. "*Mr. Wolenski will fill you in on the details.*"

"*Mr. Winthrop,*" Pauli explained as he crunched on a scone. "*We need a diesel powered, ocean going yacht with a cruising range that can reach all Caribbean ports with a minimum of refueling stops.*

At the same time, we want something easy to handle, not too big. We only have a three man crew."

"*Gentlemen,*" Nigil Winthrop politely interjected as he systematically enjoyed his morning tea, "*I'm simply embarrassed to inquire about this, but there is the matter of financing this little endeavor.*"

Christopher took over, "*Mr. Winthrop, we will pay you in cash upon completion of our order. Today, we have a bank cashier's check for $50,000.00 as a deposit.*"

"Yes, I see. Well then, gentlemen, shall we proceed!"

Sea Worthy, Inc. could deliver a boat in two weeks time. The hull, basic exterior and interior were pre-constructed. It was simply a matter of outfitting the boat with the specific equipment and comforts desired by the individual customer.

"I want state-of-the-art navigational equipment," emphasized Pauli. *"Also, VHF radio communications equipment that will enable us to send, receive and monitor communications over a large radius."*

"Yes, please go on," Nigil Winthrop was taking notes.

"We need the capability of living on this boat," added Christopher, *"so we want the very best in creature comforts."*

After several hours of considering and selecting options, Nigil Winthrop completed his check list. *"Well, gentlemen, that about does it. I'll work this up and have a complete cost breakdown for you at, shall we say, 10:00 tomorrow morning.*

This evening, however, I would be delighted if you would be my guests at one of Miami Beach's finer dining establishments, the El Bistro Cubano," offering the invitation to all three of them, but looking straight at Cindy.

"I'll ring the restaurant and make the necessary arrangements. I'll send a driver round to your hotel at about 8:00."

Turning again to Christopher and Pauli, he concluded, *"and gentlemen, It was indeed a pleasure doing business with you."*

Nigil Winthrop's smile broadened in a reserved, British sort of way as the deposit check was transferred into his hands.

The next morning, Nigil Winthrop presented Christopher and Pauli with a detailed description and price list of their order.

A small, but luxurious, 47 foot, ocean going yacht equipped with two turbocharged diesel engines that would produce cruising speeds in excess of 20 nautical miles per hour.

He further explained that they could expect a cruising range exceeding 350 nautical miles, cruising at a more economical speed of 12 nautical miles per hour.

He continued to explain that their yacht would be equipped with a state-of-the-art Global Positioning System, as well as a full complement of user friendly electronics including VHF radio communications equipment capable of monitoring weather channels for emergency bulletins.

The price, a mere $500,000.00, give or take a few thousand!

That afternoon, Christopher, Pauli and Cindy were on a plane headed back to Colorado, and their now questionable Promised Land.

Chapter Forty-Nine

Several days later, Buck charged into Sheriff Prichard's office. *"Arlan, I've been thinking, maybe we've been concentrating our investigation in the wrong area. I've been spending all my time trying to find Rob Bernstein's killer, and looking for big, dark colored, pick-up trucks."*

"What other areas you got in mind," asked Sheriff Prichard?

"Well, last night, I was going over Rob Bernstein's notes. You remember, this whole thing got started because of David Palmer's suspicion that this lady, Momma Elsie died under mysterious circumstances.

Maybe the real reason David Palmer was killed was to keep him quiet about Momma Elsie's death, rather than to stop his involvement with Rob Bernstein."

"The coroner's report just said she died of old age."

"Arlan, let's go have a talk with that coroner!"

The coroner's report did indeed list the cause of death as natural causes; but it also confirmed that there was no autopsy. Buck noted the name on the death certificate, Elsie Mae Thompson.

"Elsie Mae was born right here in these parts," the coroner was providing additional information. *"Elsie Mae Greenfield was her maiden name. Married an old boy named Daniel Thompson. They ran that ranch up there for many years. I hear she donated the ranch to that cult group!"*

"Do you remember if she had any children," asked Buck?

"I seem to recall she had maybe three. Two boys and a girl, I think. I ain't seen nor heard nothing about any of them for many years."

A check of county records revealed that Elsie Mae Thompson had two boys, Daniel, Jr. and Howard; and one girl, Sandra.

After a day or so of running their names through the computer, Buck discovered that Daniel Thompson, Jr. had retired from the U.S. Army.

"Let's get a message off to the Department of the Army and find out where Daniel Thompson, Jr. is now living."

The next day they had their answer. Daniel Thompson, Jr. had married a local girl while stationed in Germany, and had subsequently settled there after retirement.

"Let's get Daniel Thompson over here," Buck requested. *"I would like to exhume his mother's body and determine the cause of death, but I want permission from a family member to do so. It's been almost a year now since she died."*

In three days time, Daniel Thompson, Jr. was sitting in Sheriff Prichard's office.

"This is insane," he squawked. *"My mother dies and no one even informs me. It looks like someone dropped the ball around here, Sheriff. Is that the way you see it?"*

"The way I see it, son," Sheriff Prichard flatly replied, *"is that you should have spent more time with your mom! When did you last visit her? And, when was the last time you wrote her, or called her?"*

"I don't remember; two, maybe three years. Listen Sheriff, I have my own life to live."

"So, Daniel, where's your brother and sister? When did they last visit their mom? Do you have even the slightest idea as to where they are?"

"I don't know, Sheriff. I haven't heard from them in quite a few years; But, let's get back to the matter at hand. My mom has been dead for a year now. So, what became of her house in San Francisco; and what about the ranch property; and where is her trust fund? I assume she left everything to her children?"

"Sorry, son, but she either gave or left everything to the Family of God and their leader, Christopher Judah."

"This is outrageous," he fumed. "I'm going to hire a lawyer and contest the will."

"Daniel," Sheriff Prichard emphasized, "if you had spent more time with your mom, none of this would have happened."

Buck walked into the room. "Daniel Thompson, I'm FBI agent, Buck Buchanan. We have reason to believe your mom died of something other than natural causes. We would like your permission to exhume her body and perform an autopsy."

"If this Christopher Judah is responsible for my mother's death," Daniel asked, "then he would go to prison, right?"

"If we can prove it, yes."

Daniel looked away, and was thinking out loud to himself, "if this guy is convicted and goes to prison, then I'd have a better chance of overturning the will."

He looked back at Buck, and then at Sheriff Prichard. "All right, do it. You have my permission."

Chapter Fifty

The next morning, Daniel Thompson, Jr. descended upon the Promised Land with all the eloquence of a storm trooper.

"I want to see this Christopher Judah, and I want to see him now," he barked out orders through beer breath!

Christopher and Pauli were watching and listening from an upstairs window in the main house.

"Find out who this obnoxious person is, and what he wants," Christopher told Pauli.

Daniel continued his ranting and raving in a tough military manner, *"you get this guy Christopher Judah out here now!"*

"How can I help you," Pauli's low, powerful voice addressed Daniel?

Daniel sobered up a bit after viewing Pauli's demeanor. *"Yeah, well, uh, could I talk with this Christopher Judah fellow?"*

"And what business do you have here?"

"Well, my name is Daniel Thompson, and my mother, Elsie Mae Thompson owned this ranch!"

"Maybe you better come inside."

Pauli ushered Daniel Thompson into one of the rooms they had converted into an office.

"You know," volunteered Daniel, *"this used to be my room when I was a kid."*

Christopher explained the current situation, *"Mr. Thompson, your mother had not heard from you, neither from your brother or sister in more than two years. You never answered her letters. For all she knew, you were dead."*

"Yeah, well, Mr. Judah, as you can see, I'm not dead. And, as for my not writing, I have my own life to live. But now, as you can also see, I'm back, and this ranch, the house in San Fran, and the trust fund should be mine, right?"

"Mr. Thompson, your mother gave this ranch to the Family of God. She also gave us the proceeds from the sale of the house. And, she left the contents of the trust fund to us in her will. It's all legal and binding. We were the family your mom needed."

"Yeah, well, I want you to know something. I'm going to hire a lawyer and we're going to bust mom's will. All this stuff ought to be mine!"

Daniel Thompson was about to leave when a new wave of anger and boldness swept over him.

"I want you to know something else, Mr. Judah. It was suspicious the way my mom died. The sheriff and that FBI dude think maybe it was something other than just old age!"

"Your mom lived out her last days in peace, here in the Promised Land among her family," Christopher responded.

Daniel was shaking his finger at Christopher. *"Yeah, well, pretty soon we're going to know the truth. They're going to dig up mom's body and run an autopsy on it. You just might be going to jail!"*

With that, Daniel Thompson stormed out of the office, got into his rental car and scratched out of the compound, leaving gravel flying in his wake.

Christopher sat perfectly still for a long time before finally speaking in a sullen tone, *"We have to leave,"* he said. *"When will our boat be ready"?*

"According to Mr. Winthrop's schedule, it will be at least another week," answered Cindy.

"We can't wait any longer," Christopher emphasized. *"We have to leave tonight!"*

About 2:30 in the morning, Christopher backed his four wheel drive vehicle up to the back of the main house. In the darkness and stillness of the night, they carefully loaded the gold into wooden crates, and into Christopher's vehicle.

About 4:30 AM, Christopher, Pauli and Cindy climbed into the vehicle, each carrying one hastily packed bag. As quietly as possible, they eased out of the compound.

This time, there was no gathering of the Family of God. There were no speeches of exhortation and encouragement. They just disappeared into the night.

Book Four

Reaping the Whirlwind

"They sow the wind, and reap the whirlwind...."

The Prophet Hosea
From Chapter 8, verse 7

Chapter Fifty-One

Just after 7:00 that same morning, the Promised Land compound became a maze of activity.

On the grassy knoll, up by the rushing stream where Elsie Mae Thompson's body was buried, a back hoe carefully uncovered her grave under the watchful eye of the old, county coroner.

Somehow, the news of this event had been leaked. Consequently, the Promised Land was literally overrun by members of the media.

There were reporters clicking cameras and asking a multitude of questions. There were television crews taping the events for their evening news.

One of Sheriff Prichard's deputies had located Pauli's pick-up truck due to a timely tip provided by a certain female member of the Family of God.

Now, a fingerprint crew carefully dusted the big, black truck, hoping to find some sort of evidence that could link Christopher to the crimes of which he was suspected.

Arlan Prichard sat quietly on the porch of the main house, creaking back and forth in an old, antique rocker; carefully surveying the area through his aviator sun glasses.

Occasionally, a reporter would dare to ask him a question. In his usual agreeable manner, he would scowl, *"get out of my face, I don't have time for you people right now!"*

Nearby, Buck paced back and forth like a caged leopard, nervously chain smoking cigarettes.

Family of God members gathered at various vantage points, horrified by what was happening. Some of the girls were crying. Others were raising their voice in protest. A few were being interviewed by the media, and they were strongly defending Christopher Judah as a chosen messiah of God, and declaring that what was going on was a satanic plot to destroy God's work.

"So Arlan," Buck asked, *"where do you think Hawkins and this other guy, Wolenski are? You think maybe they skipped out?"*

"Don't know, could be."

"Apparently, this Wolenski fellow was the actual hit man for this outfit," suggested Buck.

"Yep, seems that way."

"Their office files seem to be intact," Buck continued to speculate. *"I can't tell whether or not any clothes are missing; and these Family of God people are no help whatsoever."*

By late morning, a truck carrying Elsie Thompson's coffin rumbled off the property, headed for Colorado Springs.

Most of the media had packed up their equipment and left.

"Arlan," Buck spoke up again. *"I think we need to have another look inside that safe. If the gold is there, Hawkins will be back. If the gold is gone, then he's gone!"*

"I'll radio my office and have them get someone up here with a blow torch," replied Sheriff Prichard. *"Apparently, None of these people know the combinations. In fact, most of them didn't even know there was a safe!"*

It took several hours for a local welder to break into the safe, but Buck's suspicions were confirmed. The gold was gone!

"Arlan, we need that autopsy expedited. I don't care if those people have to work all night!

In the meantime, ask your people to call the Department of Motor Vehicles, and find out the license plate number on Hawkins' vehicle.

Then, let's get out an All Points Bulletin on both Hawkins and Wolenski."

Chapter Fifty-Two

Christopher, Pauli and Cindy inched their way toward Miami. Figuring by now that they were wanted criminals, they avoided the Interstate Highways, traveling instead on back roads through small towns.

Not wanting to arouse any suspicion, they carefully obeyed traffic laws, especially speed limits through the small towns.

They traveled only at night, staying in out-of-the-way motels during the daytime.

Each time they stopped at a motel, the gold was laboriously lugged in and out of their room. Christopher was never far from his most precious possession.

Cindy handled check-in and check-out procedures, always under false names; and they were careful to park their vehicle in the most obscure part of the parking lot.

They also sent Cindy to pick up meals, which they ate in their rooms or on the road. In fact, Cindy took care of all such matters so that Christopher and Pauli wouldn't have to show their faces.

But, to be totally honest, Christopher also used Cindy as the errand girl because he did not want to leave the gold! He was quite paranoid these days, and didn't know who he could, or could not trust!

"Can we trust Cindy," Christopher asked Pauli one day when she was out shopping for food? *"As you know, she's not directly guilty of any wrongdoing."*

"Yes, I believe we can," answered Pauli. *"She wants to enjoy the benefits of the gold."* But, Pauli also had other motives for giving Cindy a vote of confidence.

Every time they crossed the border into a new state: Oklahoma, Texas, Arkansas, Mississippi, Alabama and finally Florida; Pauli made one specific stop, to steal a local license plate to replace the one currently on their vehicle.

After four nights of continuous, tedious driving, they finally arrived in Miami. An hour later, they checked into a Miami Beach hotel, physically, mentally and emotionally exhausted.

While jet setters and beach goers enjoyed the playgrounds of Miami Beach, Christopher, Pauli and Cindy slept for ten hours.

"Good morning," came a cheery voice through the phone. *"This is the offices of Sea Worthy, Inc., builder of the finest yachts ever to sail a sea!"*

"Mr. Winthrop, please," came the other voice.

"And, who may I say is calling?"

"Brad Hawkins."

After a short pause, Nigil Winthrop came on the line, *"Top O the morning to you, Mr. Hawkins. I have wonderful news for you. Due to the competency of my excellent staff, we'll be completing your order by this afternoon, almost two full days ahead of schedule."*

"As you British would say, that's splendid!" Christopher felt encouraged as he held the phone and shared the news. *"I'll be at your office around noon with a cashier's check,"* he concluded.

"Always a pleasure, Mr. Hawkins. Always a pleasure doing business with fine gentlemen like yourself."

"Oh, Mr. Hawkins," Nigil Winthrop exclaimed, remembering a matter of unfinished business, *"there's just one more small detail."*

"Yes," answered Christopher.

"The name, Mr. Hawkins. What name do you wish to have on your yacht? As part of our personal services here at Sea Worthy, we provide an eloquent, calligraphic plaque in the colors of your choice with which you may display the name of your vessel."

Christopher was caught completely off guard. He had to earnestly think about Mr. Winthrop's question for a minute. With all the current turmoil, naming the boat hadn't even crossed his mind.

Finally, he responded, *"we'll just name it: THE CHRISTOPHER."*

"Jolly good name, Mr. Hawkins, jolly good name," chuckled Nigil Winthrop. *"I seem to recall another chap named Christopher who sailed these waters some years ago."*

"Yes, well, good day Mr. Winthrop."

Chapter Fifty-Three

Meanwhile, Buck Buchanan's manhunt had bogged down. They did have their first concrete evidence in the case. The autopsy confirmed that Momma Elsie died as a result of arsenic poisoning. However, it had now been four days since they exhumed her body and there was no trace whatsoever of Christopher and Pauli.

"I want to see that FBI man," the voice demanded.

"Hey, I remember you," one of Sheriff Prichard's deputies was responding to the voice. *"You're the lady who tipped me off about the location of Wolenski's pick-up."*

"*Congratulations,*" she responded, "*but right now, I want to talk with that FBI man!*"

"*May I ask what about?*"

"*You must be kidding,*" she sarcastically stated! "*Where have you been for the last four days?*"

Buck was listening from the doorway of Sheriff Prichard's office. "*Young lady, would you mind stepping into the office.*"

"*I'm FBI agent, Buck Buchanan, and this is Sheriff Arlan Prichard.*"

"*I already know who you are!*"

"*And, who might you be, young lady?*"

"*Naomi.*"

"*Naomi who?*"

"*Just Naomi is good enough; and I've got some information you need!*"

"*O.K., I'm all ears,*" Buck replied. "*What kind of information do you have?*"

"*Information about Christopher Judah; but first, I want $5,000.00.*"

"*This ain't no bank,*" piped in Sheriff Prichard!

"*Listen,*" said Naomi, "*I know the FBI pays for information, and I want $5,000.00 or I'm not saying another word.*"

"*And, why is this money so important,*" asked Buck?

"*I need to get out of this place,*" she explained. "*Nobody in the Family of God has any money. We gave everything we had to Christopher; and every nickel we made was sent straight to the office!*"

"Our local Crime Stoppers account can offer $1,000.00 for information leading to an arrest and conviction," Sheriff Prichard was explaining to Buck.

"You can forget that," said Naomi. *"I don't have time to wait around here to see if you can catch them!"*

Buck briefly glanced at Sheriff Prichard as if he was waiting to receive permission for something. *"O.K.,"* said Arlan, *"we'll give you $1,000.00."*

"I want $1,000.00 and a first class airline ticket to San Francisco, and that's my final offer!"

"Done," said Buck!

Naomi nonchalantly located the most comfortable chair in the office and requested a cup of coffee. *"Cream and sugar please, and two of those donuts."*

"First of all," she began, *"you're not looking for two people. You're looking for three: Christopher Judah, Paul Wolenski and Cindy Palmer."*

"Cindy Palmer," interrupted Buck, *"is she related to David Palmer?"*

"Used to be his wife," answered Naomi. *"Now she's supposed to be Christopher's woman. I used to be his woman before Miss Teen Queen Maria came along. After she died, that little wench, Cindy wormed her way into his bed."*

"Could we get back to the information," Buck requested?

"O.K., O.K., relax! About 10, maybe 12 days ago," she continued, *"Christopher, Pauli and Cindy flew to Miami."*

"How do you know that?"

"I make it my business to know things! Anyway, about four days ago, just before they made their getaway from the Promised Land, I saw a road map on Pauli's desk. He had it marked with a highlighter all the way to Miami."

"Yes, go on."

"That's all I know," reported Naomi.

"That's all the information you have?"

"It's more than you had before I walked in here. Now, I want my thousand dollars and my first class airline ticket!"

Immediately, Buck was on the phone, alerting FBI headquarters in Miami. Afterwards, he booked himself and Arlan on the first available flight headed for Miami.

About 45 minutes later as Naomi was leaving the office, Buck asked one more question, *"So, Naomi, what do you think of Mr. Christopher Judah now?"*

"He's a jerk," she said, *"pausing to take the last donut."*

"And, why do you say that?"

"Because he didn't take me with him!"

Chapter Fifty-Four

Pauli and Christopher spent the morning shopping for supplies and equipment. Cindy just spent the morning shopping.

One old salt of a seaman offered some advice, *"I wouldn't be striking out for a few days if I were you. There's a tropical storm 750 miles south/southeast of here. Right now, the winds are about 60 miles per hour, and it's headed west toward the gulf, but these things can be tricky. I've seen them change directions and pick up steam, just like that,"* as he snapped his finger!

"Is the storm a problem," Christopher asked later?

"It poses no threat to us," Pauli replied. *"We'll set a course for Cay San Pueblo, and according to my calculations, if we cruise at around 12 knots, with three refueling stops, we should be there in about three and a half days."*

"You don't think we should wait a day or so, and watch the storm," he asked?

"Christopher, can we afford to wait? We don't know how close the FBI is on our trail. Besides, I've been in storms all over the Great Lakes, if it comes to that!"

"How far is Cay San Pueblo from the United States," Christopher continued to inquire?

"As the crow flies, it's about 700 miles from Miami," answered Pauli, *"but since we have to avoid Cuba, and make a few refueling stops, it will end up being more than 900 miles."*

That afternoon, Christopher, Pauli and Cindy were checking out their new boat.

Cindy was enamored with the polished teak wood, gleaming brass and plush accommodations. Nigil Winthrop was especially anxious to personally show Cindy the luxury features aboard their vessel.

Christopher was especially interested in the yacht's security features. Sea Worthy had installed an elaborate combination safe with a computerized locking system.

Pauli listened intently as Sea Worthy employees explained and demonstrated on-board navigational, weather and communications equipment.

Later, Cindy impatiently listened while a Sea Worthy employee showed her how to operate the appliances in the yacht's galley.

"A millionaire should not have to be a scullery mate," she thought to herself.

For the next three hours, Sea Worthy employees watched and periodically offered advice as Pauli maneuvered up and down one of the canals that separates the City of Miami from Miami Beach.

"Piece of cake," Pauli confidently exclaimed. *"This baby handles like a dream!"*

Meanwhile, in an office across town, Buck Buchanan and Sheriff Prichard were fervently working with local FBI agents.

"Being that they came here to Miami," said one agent, *"it would appear that they intend to leave the country."*

"Buck," said another, *"we've started a check of airline computers, cruise ship rosters and charter boat bookings. Nothing so far,"* he added. *"This is a big city. It's going to take some time."*

"As we speak," said yet another agent, *"photos of this guy, Christopher Judah are being circulated to law enforcement agencies all over the Miami area."*

"Buck," said the agent in charge, *"we're working on an arrangement with the Coast Guard and local law enforcement agencies. Just as soon as we can get things organized and coordinated, we'll seal off all the exits out of the city."*

"Now comes the hard part," said Buck.

"Yeah, I know what you mean," Arlan responded. *"Waiting!"*

"I feel so helpless sitting around here waiting," added Buck. *"I feel like going out to the airport and walking around through the terminal looking for them!"*

Christopher and Pauli made one final trip to their hotel room. For the last time, they loaded the gold into Christopher's vehicle, and subsequently into the yacht's safe.

It's a good thing they had the gold in indistinguishable wooden crates. Any thief stumbling across their path would have pulled off a career job.

They spent their first night aboard THE CHRISTOPHER.

Pauli stayed up late, carefully studying navigational charts, plotting each leg of their journey, and then checking it and rechecking it all over again.

Christopher seemed preoccupied, and didn't seem to be interested in Cindy; so she just lounged around on the sun deck, drinking champagne until about midnight.

"How long did you say it would take us to get there?" Christopher had come onto the bridge and was asking some of the same questions again.

"About three and one half days," Pauli answered, *"and being that we're departing bright and early this morning, we should arrive in Cay San Pueblo prior to dark on our third day out."*

"Did you take refueling stops into consideration in your calculations," Christopher inquired, trying to make sure Pauli had taken care of all the details?

"Yes, I'm allowing three hours per fuel stop."

"Aren't you going to be a little tired trying to maintain such a schedule," Christopher inquired again?

"I'll need help from you and Cindy," he responded. *"Both of you will have to stand limited watches; but don't worry, I'll show you exactly what to do!"*

Early the next morning, they were all scurrying about, making ready to get under way.

Around 6:30, Cindy came back to the boat after picking up breakfast; looking like she had seen a ghost.

"Sheriff Prichard and that FBI agent were at the restaurant having breakfast," she explained excitedly!

239

"I told you we didn't have time to wait around here and watch that silly, little, tropical storm," Pauli emphasized! *"I would rather take my chances against a storm than against those guys!"*

"All right, I'm convinced," said Christopher, *"let's get out of here!"*

At 7:00 sharp, THE CHRISTOPHER cruised out of Miami. They were about one half hour ahead of the combined effort by Miami law enforcement agencies to seal off the exits!

Chapter Fifty-Five

Buck's manhunt had continued through the night, but to no avail. There were no reservations, no bookings, nothing under the names, Christopher Judah, Brad Hawkins, Paul Wolenski or Cindy Palmer.

"They could have used an alias," one of the agents suggested; but so far, no one had recognized Christopher's photo which was being circulated all over the city.

Police patrol cars were on the lookout for Christopher's vehicle, but it had been abandoned the previous evening in one of Miami's lower class neighborhoods. It was now stripped and indistinguishable.

As morning dawned, Buck was weary and frustrated, just barely staying awake due to the caffeine from multiple cups of strong, black coffee. Nearby was his usual disgusting mountain of cigarette butts and ashes, half in the ashtray and half all over the desk.

"Let's grab some breakfast, Arlan. I'm exhausted, and I need some nourishment!" They didn't see Cindy as she stopped dead in her tracks and momentarily stared at them before quickly leaving the restaurant.

Suddenly, an idea flashed into Buck's mind. He leaped to his feet with new vigor, from somewhere, and hurried to a phone. *"Get every available agent on the phones,"* he shouted. *"Check every brokerage house in Miami. Find out if anyone has recently changed gold into currency."*

By 10:00 AM, Buck had his answer. One of the local brokerage firms in Miami's financial district had changed almost a half million dollars of gold into currency; and had subsequently issued a cashier's check to a Sea Worthy, Inc., builder of luxury yachts.

"Arlan," Buck shouted, *"they've bought themselves a boat!"*

Twenty minutes later, a rumpled Buck Buchanan was questioning Nigil Winthrop.

"Obviously, sir, I didn't have even the foggiest notion that they were the criminal sort," explained a nervous Nigil Winthrop. *"Had I suspected anything fishy, I certainly would have alerted the authorities."*

"Isn't it a bit unusual for someone to pay $500,000.00 in cash for a boat," asked Sheriff Prichard?

"In my line of work, Sheriff, we deal almost exclusively with people who, shall we say, are rather well-heeled!"

For the next hour, Buck quizzed an impatient and agitated Nigil Winthrop regarding Christopher and his companion's likely departure time; as well as the capabilities and capacities of the yacht that Sea Worthy had prepared for them.

Nigil breathed a sigh of relief as Buck finally got up to leave. Nearby, the serving of English breakfast tea, scones and marmalade lay untouched.

Several hours later, Buck and Arlan were discussing the situation with Coast Guard officials.

"My guess is, they're likely headed for Cay San Pueblo," suggested one Lieutenant.

"If they left last night," added a Chief Petty Officer, "given the speed of that type of vessel, they could be more than 200 miles out."

"Could we get a plane in the air and intercept them," asked Arlan?

"I would advise against it," answered the Lieutenant. "They're probably in international waters by now; and the truth is, we don't know for sure where they're headed.

There are over 700 islands in the Bahama's chain," he explained. *"Unfortunately, there are many places to hide! It would be like looking for a needle in a haystack.*

Besides, we're monitoring a tropical storm just south of Jamaica, which could potentially turn into a hurricane!

I'll alert the authorities in Nassau. Maybe we can apprehend them during one of their fuel stops."

Later that evening, Buck and Arlan were having dinner. *"Buck,"* asked Arlan, *"if they make it to Cay San Pueblo, can we ask the government down there to pick them up and send them back?"*

Buck had a disgusted look on his face. *"I'm afraid not, Arlan. The United States doesn't have an extradition arrangement with the Cay San Pueblo government. With a few well placed bribes, they could secure their future there."*

Buck paused for a few minutes between sips of coffee, and then continued, *"the truth is, Arlan, we're not even sure they're headed for Cay San Pueblo. But, even if they are, and even if we knew it, there's not a thing we could do about it!"*

Buck finished his third cup of coffee, got up to leave and added one last concluding comment, *"Arlan, I'm afraid we've lost this one!"*

Chapter Fifty-Six

It was an absolutely beautiful morning on board THE CHRISTOPHER. The sea was calm except for an occasional light, salt spray, the water was a sparkling, deep blue and the sun was warm and bright.

On this initial leg of their journey, they were cruising southeast toward Andros Island in the Bahama's chain.

Early that evening as the sun was setting, they cruised around the northern end of the island and headed down the eastern side.

They continued southeast toward their first refueling stop in George Town on Great Exuma Island.

It was around 10:30 the next morning when they arrived at George Town. Christopher didn't sleep well during the night. He was uneasy about being, as he put it, *"in the middle of the sea in the middle of the night."*

In addition, he wasn't yet accustomed to the rolling and pitching of traveling on the sea.

Three and one half hours later, after a timely refueling stop, they cruised out of George Town and continued heading in a southeasterly direction toward their next scheduled stop at Matthew Town on Great Inagua Island.

About an hour after they were refueled and gone, an untimely radio message from Nassau arrived at the George Town police headquarters.

Things operate at a slower pace here in the islands!

Meanwhile, Pauli was keeping a close eye on the weather equipment and monitoring every weather report. The tropical storm had shifted position, just slightly, and was now about 100 miles south of the stretch of sea separating Cay San Pueblo and Jamaica.

"If the storm will just sit there," thought Pauli, *"we might encounter a little rain and some choppy seas, but we should easily make it into Cay San Pueblo."*

"We're right on schedule and making good time," Pauli cheerfully announced to everyone!

But, Christopher was edgy. He paced back and forth throughout the cabin, around the sun deck and up to the bridge.

He was relieved about being out of the grasp of Buck Buchanan and Sheriff Arlan Prichard, but he was still uneasy and unsteady about being on the sea.

Periodically, he would relax for a little while and meditate about weaving his way into the fiber of Cay San Pueblo society; and about establishing a new Promised Land.

Cindy wasn't concerned at all. She lay on the sun deck, considerably more unclothed than clothed, soaking up the warm sun.

It didn't seem to matter that her nakedness was exposed to both men. Why bother with restraints or act spiritual now. They had it made!

The fact was, she and Pauli had recently started their own affair. If Christopher knew about it, he hadn't said anything.

"I don't think he cares one way or the other," she thought. *"Lately, he hasn't been the least bit interested in me."* In fact, she had even noticed him eyeing the young boys before they left the Promised Land!

"Oh well, who cares," she thought as she turned over to tan the other side. *"If necessary, I can take care of both of them."*

She started dreaming again about white sandy beaches, crystal blue lagoons, nightclubs, casinos, tall refreshing cocktails and steel drum bands.

Early the next morning, after making good time during the night, they cruised into Matthew Town.

"Smooth as silk," exclaimed Pauli. *"I told you that storm wouldn't be a problem. It's still just sitting there, like a wimp, in the same location."*

But, in Matthew Town, they encountered a different problem. They couldn't find anyone to help them with refueling.

"Some sort of a holiday," volunteered one lonesome tourist. *"Anyway,"* he continued, *"things don't always operate on schedule down here."*

"We've got to have fuel," fumed Pauli. *"Where can I find someone to help us?"*

"If we're going to be here for a while, can I go see the flamingoes," asked Cindy?

"What on earth are you talking about," an irritated Christopher asked?

"It says right here in my tourist guide that Inagua National Park has more than 50,000 flamingoes."

"May I remind you," Christopher said in a scolding voice, *"we are not tourists! We're fugitives! Do you understand that?"*

"Well, pardon me," Cindy exclaimed as she disappeared into the cabin!

Six hours later, after practically bribing an attendant, they finally got refueled and underway again. *"We're behind schedule,"* said Pauli, *"and we still have to make one more stop!"*

Interestingly, a message that had been radioed from Nassau lay on the island police chief's desk. It alerted local police to be on the lookout for two men, one woman and a yacht named THE CHRISTOPHER.

But, the alert wouldn't be implemented until tomorrow. Today was a holiday!

They headed south through the windward passage that separates Haiti and Cuba; then turning southeast, they headed for the seaport town of St. Marc; arriving there, unfortunately, in the middle of the night!

The place was completely shut down except for a few sleazy bars. They remained on the boat and tried to get some sleep. It was four and one half hours later before they were able to refuel.

"That stupid holiday in Matthew Town really cost us," emphasized Pauli, while they were being refueled. *"Right now, we're way behind schedule!"*

"How much longer until we get to Cay San Pueblo." asked Christopher?

"I'm not sure," Pauli answered sharply. *"Those two delays fouled up our schedule. The best I can calculate, we still have about 18 hours of cruising ahead of us!"*

"That means we won't arrive until after midnight," a concerned Christopher responded! *"And, what about the storm?"*

"Christopher," Pauli stressed, *"it's still just a tropical storm, and it's still just sitting there. It poses no threat to us!"*

It was evident that Pauli was tired!

"Is everything O.K., Pauli," Christopher asked? *"We could stop and rest for a day."*

"Listen Christopher," Pauli responded with irritation in his voice, *"Haiti is one of those volatile places where you don't stay any longer than you have to!"*

Christopher couldn't argue with that. Since maneuvering into the refueling station, they had become a spectacle for a growing number of desperate looking people, seemingly longing for a taste of their luxury.

He had also noticed a few unsavory looking characters in the crowd, seemingly sizing them up for a potential robbery.

"Is there somewhere else we could rest for a day," he asked Pauli?

"There's always Cuba," Pauli snapped! *"We would either be blown out of the water by Cuban gunboats; or detained for about six months while they figured out the most advantageous way to send us back into the waiting arms of the FBI!"*

A few minutes later though, Pauli put on his strong face and tempered his voice, *"Hey, Christopher, don't worry! Everything is under control. This is our last leg. We're going to make it!"*

But, to be sure, Pauli would be glad to get into Cay San Pueblo! Due to Christopher and Cindy's limited knowledge and experience in navigation, he had managed precious little sleep in the past 72 hours.

Chapter Fifty-Seven

It was almost 9:00 in the morning when THE CHRISTOPHER departed St. Marc. Pauli steered north of Ile de la Gonave and then headed southwest in the direction of Jamaica.

Early that evening, they rounded the southwestern tip of Haiti, turned due south, and headed straight for Cay San Pueblo, still at least nine hours away.

The Caribbean seas were a bit choppy now, and a little rain had begun to fall. THE CHRISTOPHER seemed very much alone. There were no other boats in sight, and Haiti was fading fast in their background.

In front of them were wicked looking skies, but Pauli plowed onward toward their destination.

A little debate surfaced as Christopher and Cindy voiced their concerns. *"Are you sure we should be doing this,"* Cindy asked? *"The sea is getting rougher,"* added Christopher, *"and I don't like the look of that sky!"*

"May I inquire as to your alternatives," stated Pauli? *"Behind us is the desperation and political unrest of Haiti, and in front of us is freedom!"*

"I would also like to remind you," Pauli argued, *"that all we're facing is the fringes of a little tropical storm. Just find something stationary and hold on! I'll get you safely into Cay San Pueblo!"*

Unfortunately, around 9:00, just after darkness had totally surrounded them, they monitored a frightening weather bulletin. The tropical storm had been upgraded to a hurricane!

Hurricane Joscalyn, as she was now called, had rapidly increased in fury and was packing winds of 125 miles per hour.

"Pauli," asked a frightened Christopher, *"What are we going to do now?"*

"The storm is still just sitting there," Pauli responded. *"As long as it's not moving toward us, we can still make it into Cay San Pueblo. We can find shelter in one of the coves on the north coast and wait out the storm. If can't last much longer."*

"How much further is the island," asked Christopher?

"No more than seventy, maybe eighty miles," Pauli answered. *"I'm going to increase our speed to 20 knots."*

The seas had become much heavier now, and even though Pauli increased the speed in excess of 20 knots, the going somehow seemed slower.

Then, around 10:00, it happened! The weather bulletin they were dreading was broadcast over the ship's radio.

Hurricane Joscalyn was on the move! She was roaring over the open sea, traveling at the incredible speed of 40 miles per hour, and headed straight toward Cay San Pueblo!

Their roomy, luxury yacht all of a sudden seemed small and vulnerable. It began to creak and groan as the surging seas became heavier. Sheets of rain periodically buffeted the windows of the bridge.

"We're not going to make it to Cay San Pueblo," Pauli's voice was loud and excited as he finally reached this decision. *"Even traveling at top speed, the strength of the storm would intercept us about 10 miles out!"*

"Let's turn the boat around," yelled Christopher!

Pauli had to make a quick decision. He could turn around, but the hurricane might overtake them before they made it back to shelter in Haiti.

He definitely could not turn the boat due east. The closest islands were so far away that they would run out of fuel.

"I'm going to turn due west and run for shelter on the north coast of Jamaica." he shouted over the storm!

Meanwhile, Cindy was huddled below in the cabin, bracing herself in the rough seas, holding tightly to whatever fixture she could grasp hold of, trying to keep from smashing herself against the bulkheads.

Just as Pauli was preparing to turn due west and run for the north coast of Jamaica, she suddenly remembered leaving her watch on the sun deck.

It was a brand new, very expensive, diamond studded watch that she had begged Christopher to buy her in Miami.

She debated in her mind regarding what to do. Impulsively, she struggled to her feet and headed for the hatch. Once outside, she was forced to crawl on her hands and knees because of the wind and rain.

"There it is," she said out loud. The watch was lodged in a corner, a bit wet and periodically pounding against the bulkhead.

"I'm glad it's water proof and shock resistant," she said as she stretched forth one hand to retrieve the watch, while shielding her face from the stinging rain with the other hand!

On the bridge, Pauli had steered the boat into a 90 degree turn. Now, the storm was no longer battling their bow, but was headed full force toward their port side!

Cindy crawled toward the ladder leading up to the bridge. *"I'm not going back to the cabin and endure this ordeal alone,"* she decided.

Suddenly, and without warning, Cindy's breath was momentarily taken away as THE CHRISTOPHER dropped, seemingly into a deep cavern in the path of an oncoming 25 foot wave.

Startled and wild eyed, she struggled to her feet and with wobbly legs attempted to run the remaining distance to the ladder.

It was too late! The huge wave crashed over the boat, tearing her grasp from the handrail and hurling her overboard, some 20 feet into the open sea!

Her cries for help were totally drowned out by the roar of the storm!

Inside the bridge, Christopher and Pauli were unaware of Cindy's dilemma. They were in a fight of their own, exerting an all out effort to steady themselves and hold the boat on course.

They were so busy that they didn't hear the latest weather bulletin. Hurricane Joscalyn had shifted directions again, just slightly. She was now headed directly for them!

Hour after hour the storm raged on, increasing in fury! The very structure of their boat sounded as if it would be torn apart! Huge waves continued to crash over the boat!

About 2:00 in the morning, Hurricane Joscalyn ripped the ship's wheel from the hands of a totally exhausted Pauli!

He and Christopher bounced and rolled around the floor of the bridge as Hurricane Joscalyn freely pitched and tossed the yacht in the raging sea!

Finally, they managed to grasp hold of something stationary and temporarily steady themselves!

"Get this boat under control," Christopher screamed at Pauli!

A weary and forlorn Pauli looked back at Christopher and weakly said, *"I don't think we're going to make it!"*

For the first time in the more than three years that he had followed Brad Hawkins, alias Christopher Judah, he saw a strange, different look on his face.

All the masks were off now! It was the unmistakable look of not being in control!

Chapter Fifty-Eight

The Marine Corps patrol didn't expect what they found on the beach the next day. In the aftermath of Hurricane Joscalyn, they were checking for storm damage on the perimeter of the Guantanamo Bay U.S. Naval Station in its unlikely location on the southeastern coast of Cuba.

As they made temporary repairs along the perimeter, they were surprised to find a body washed up on the beach. Even more surprising was the fact that this body was wearing one of those highly protective life jackets designed to hold your head out of the water, even if you're unconscious!

Upon closer examination, they had the answer to this drowning victim's demise. His pockets: trousers, shirt and jacket, were stuffed with more than 18 pounds of gold bars and gold coins.

18 pounds of gold had literally pulled his head under the water!

By the next morning, the dead man's photograph and fingerprints had been relayed to the Coast Guard, and subsequently, to the FBI.

It was a positive identification. The dead man was identified as Bradley Eugene Hawkins!

For several days, assorted pieces of debris continued to wash up on the shore.

As to the whereabouts of Cindy Palmer and Paul Wolenski, their bodies were never found!

After receiving the news at the Miami FBI office, Buck and Sheriff Prichard were dispatched to Guantanamo Bay via a special Coast Guard aircraft.

They both requested to view the body, primarily to satisfy themselves that the dead man was indeed Brad Hawkins.

Afterwards, they were escorted to the place where Brad's body had been found.

As they strolled along the beach, Buck periodically retrieved and examined pieces of debris.

He called Arlan's attention to one piece that was particularly interesting. It was a jagged piece of wood, somewhat battered by the sea; but clearly recognizable was the decoratively painted name of a luxury yacht: THE CHRISTOPHER!

Before climbing back into the Marine Corps vehicle and heading back to the headquarters building, Buck took one more long look at the sea.

"You know, Arlan," he began, *"somewhere out there, whether in deep water or shallow, I don't know!*

Whether visible on the sea floor or hidden among craggy rocks, I don't know!

Whether one day discoverable by treasure hunters or not, I don't know!

But somewhere out there under this sparkling blue Caribbean is a state-of-the-art, computerized, combination safe containing a million dollars in gold!

Arlan Prichard's starched, sheriff's department issue shirt was almost completely wet with sweat. He removed his trooper hat and wiped his brow in the hot Cuban sun. *"Let's go home, Buck!"*

"So are the ways of everyone who is greedy for gain; it takes away the life of its owners."

The Wisdom of Solomon
Proverbs, Chapter 1, verse 19

Bradley Eugene Hawkins' body was shipped back to Cartersville, at government expense.

It was buried close by the graves of Belinda Sue Hawkins and Nellie Hawkins, at the town's expense.

None of his relatives were interested in viewing the body for identification. They just took the government's word for it.

Mayor Smiley worked hard to play down several days of media fanfare, trying hard to salvage Cartersville's good name.

Exactly two people were present at the occasion of Bradley's burial. Both were grave diggers!

"....all flesh is as grass, and all the glory of man as the flower of the grass. The grass withers, and its flower falls away, but the word of the Lord endures forever."

> First Epistle of the Apostle Peter
> Chapter 1, verse 24

Book Five

Epilogue

"....I am the way, the truth, and the life. No one comes to the Father except through me."

>Jesus Christ
>The Gospel According to John
>Chapter 14, verse 6

Chapter Fifty-Nine

It was Sunday afternoon. Ida Prichard was scurrying about the kitchen, putting the final touches on her meal for the gathering of the Prichard clan. Such gatherings had become pretty much of a Sunday afternoon tradition.

A horde of kids ran roughshod through the house, slowing down temporarily after each threat of, *"this is my last warning!"*

Daughters and daughters-in-law worked along side Ida, periodically transporting full platters and deep dishes of scrumptious looking food to the huge, homemade picnic table.

There was baked catfish, southern fried chicken, bar-be-que beef ribs, black-eyed peas, green beans, corn on the cob, sweet potatoes, homemade biscuits, corn fritters and multiple pitchers of iced tea, not to mention the key lime pie.

On this particular Sunday, there was a place setting for a guest; specifically for the person of one soon to be retired FBI agent.

Pastor Buddy Prichard listened as his big brother, Arlan and Buck Buchanan talked about the deception and treachery they had uncovered in the Family of God. He listened even more intently as they recounted the events of the past week.

In the past, he had tried to reach out to various members of the Family of God when they came into Roper. So far, he had made no progress. They were fiercely committed to Christopher Judah, and staunchly saturated with his doctrines.

All attempts to reach out to them in the past had resulted in heated debates, rebuttals and rebukes from the cult members.

Now perhaps, there would be a fresh, new opportunity. He would pray about the matter.

His thoughts were interrupted by his older brother. *"Buddy,"* Arlan said, while gnawing on a bar-be-que rib, *"now's the time to reach out to these kids. They're confused, they're hurt and they've been betrayed. They have no direction for their lives."*

Meanwhile, back at the Promised Land, things were in complete disarray.

Some Family of God members refused to believe the reports of Christopher's death. *"Can't you see,"* they declared, *"it's a trick!" "It's all a lie perpetrated by the government to destroy us? Christopher will return. He's been away before, and he's always come back!"*

Others were almost emotional basket cases. They just wept and wept from the hurt, confusion and betrayal.

Many began to quietly pack their few belongings and leave. For several days, the sides of the highway were filled with young men and women trying to hitchhike rides.

Some went back to families, who were still willing to take them back!

Others hoped they could get back into school.

A precious few were fortunate enough to return to jobs.

Many had no idea of where to go; they were just leaving.

By the end of the month, the population of the Promised Land had dwindled to 125.

Sadly, this group had nowhere to go. They had burned their bridges behind them for the hope of eternity!

For a while, they could continue living at the ranch; but, it was just a matter of time until the will was overturned, and ownership reverted to Daniel Thompson, Jr.

Those who remained in the Promised Land recognized that the end was near. Consequently, their once thriving industries came to a grinding halt.

There were no potential messiahs to assume leadership. Consequently, there was no more teaching, no singing and no sounds of musical instruments in the air.

There was no longer a cause or purpose for their lives. Their stanch commitments had been reduced to ashes. They had given their all to Christopher Judah and the Family of God, and in the end, there was nothing to show for it.

There was no joy in the Promised Land. There was however, depression, bordering on despair!

Their days settled into the pattern of mundanely providing for their daily subsistence.

"Do not put your trust in princes, nor in a son of man, in whom there is no help. His spirit departs, he returns to his earth; **IN THAT VERY DAY HIS PLANS PERISH.**"

Psalm 146, verses 3-4

Chapter Sixty

The Family of God, if you could still call them that, was awakened by the pounding of a hammer. First, it was over there, then closer, and finally, right outside their living quarters.

Several of them sleepily wandered out to see what was happening.

Pastor Buddy Prichard was putting up flyers! Professionally printed, ivory colored flyers with bright red trim and bold blue letters. As the Family of God looked around the compound, the flyers were everywhere.

One young lady rubbed the sleep out of her eyes and read the flyer:

Foundations Of The Christian Faith

A class designed for the
reeducation of former
Family of God members

If you're unsure about your eternal future, come and join us at 9:00 AM this Sunday in the education building of the Roper Christian Fellowship, located at 441 Aspen Way Road.

Everyone Is Welcome !

When Pastor Buddy was preparing the flyer, he struggled with the wordage. He was tempted to cleverly word the flyer so as to mask the real purpose of the class, lest he offend them.

But, then he decided, *"no, I'm going to come at them straightforward! There's no merit in adding deception upon deception!"*

So, now it was Sunday morning. Pastor Buddy and his wife, Suzzane arrived at the small, family oriented church earlier than usual.

After setting up the chairs, they walked throughout the classroom, praying and interceding for the Family of God members.

Would this time be different? Would they finally be able to reach these kids?

At 8:30, they organized and laid out the 100 lesson outlines they had prepared for the first class.

At 8:40, they set out styrofoam cups, napkins, paper plates and plastic forks, then continued praying.

At 8:45, they prepared the coffee maker and set out the cream and sugar.

At 8:50, they turned the coffee maker on. Soon, the aroma of fresh brewed coffee filled the whole classroom.

At 8:55, they opened boxes of pastries, and then, they waited!

9:00 came; there was no one in sight! They kept praying.

At 9:05, Suzzane said, *"I guess they're not coming!"*

"Let's wait five more minutes," said Buddy Prichard. *"Just keep praying!"*

At 9:10, they heard a noise in the parking lot. One of the squeaky, old vans owned by the Family of God pulled to a stop.

Pastor Buddy could hear his heart beating. Suzzane was noticeably nervous. They waited in the classroom, trying to remain calm.

A few minutes later, three weary looking, shabbily dressed, emotionally drained souls poked their heads through the door.

They chose not to stay for the worship service, leaving immediately after the class; but it was a start! They did manage to consume a goodly number of the pastries!

As the weeks turned into a month, class attendance steadily increased. The second week, there were 9. The third week, 17; and the fourth week, attendance exploded to 60.

One by one, they accepted Jesus Christ as their Messiah.

Water baptism services were conducted at the ranch each Saturday afternoon.

On Wednesday evenings, Pastor Buddy came to the ranch to conduct an open discussion group where they could ask questions. Many were filled with the Holy Spirit.

As the classes progressed, little by little they were transformed by the renewing of their minds with the truth of God's word.

As the living, powerful word of God was continually implanted into their souls, emotional healing began to take place.

New direction and guidance for their lives began to spring forth by the leading of the Holy Spirit.

One Sunday morning, a visitor attended the class. He also had a Bible and a notebook, but was clearly distinguishable from the others. His presence caused whispering among the class and glances in his direction.

He sat on the back row trying to be as inconspicuous as possible, but he didn't fool anyone. It was the clearly recognizable, unmistakable figure, minus the cigarettes, of one recently retired FBI agent!

The End

....but please continue to the next page!

Jesus said....
I Am the Way

Jesus gave us this warning, *"....Take heed that you not be deceived. For many will come in My name, saying, I am He, and the time has drawn near. Therefore, DO NOT GO AFTER THEM!"* (Luke 21:8).

But, the Bible also gives us this invitation, *"But as many as received Him* (Jesus Christ), *to them He gave the right to become children of God, even to those who believe in His name!"* (John 1:12).

Have you received Jesus Christ as your Savior? He died for the sins of the whole world, that we might have a right standing before God, *"For He* (God, the Father) *made Him* (Jesus Christ) *who knew no sin to be sin for us, that we might become the righteousness of God in Him."* (2 Corinthians 5:21).

There's no need to look for a messiah anywhere else! Romans 4:12 says, speaking of Jesus Christ, *"Nor is there salvation in any other, for there is no other name under heaven given among men by which we must be saved!"*

Don't waste your time trying to clean yourself up, and become acceptable in God's sight. Only the blood of Jesus can cleanse you from sin, *"To Him who loved us and washed us from our sins in His own blood."* (Revelation 1:5).

And, don't bother with trying to become godlike. Titus 3:4-5 clearly tells us, *"....the kindness and the love of God our Savior toward man appeared, NOT BY WORKS OF RIGHTEOUSNESS WHICH WE HAVE DONE, but according to His mercy He saved us...."*

This should go without saying, but just in case, I'll include it. YOU DEFINITELY CANNOT BECOME A GOD! God Himself declares, *"....Before Me there was no God formed, Nor shall there be after Me. I, even I, am the Lord, and besides Me there is no Savior...!"* (Isaiah 43:10-11).

You can only come to God just as you are, and accept his forgiveness and cleansing through Jesus Christ.

Would you like to do that? If so, here's a prayer you can pray to invite Jesus Christ into your life. Don't be ashamed or embarrassed. Pray out loud! Pray directly to God!

Heavenly Father, I come before you in the name of your only begotten son, Jesus Christ.

I come to receive Jesus as my Savior; and be cleansed from sin by the blood that Jesus shed for me when he was crucified on the cross.

Heavenly Father, I also believe that you raised Jesus Christ from the dead. He is alive now; and he is willing to come into my life and dwell within me, changing me into a new creation.

Lord Jesus, I personally invite you to come into my life. Cleanse me with your blood! Wash my sin away! Give me a right standing before God! I Thank you, Lord Jesus, for coming into my life.

From this time forth in my life, I declare that you, Lord Jesus, are my Savior, my God and my Lord! Amen!

Just one more page......

Now, please listen to me carefully. As these end times continue to unfold, you will come into contact with all kinds of clever, and sometimes, seemingly logical deception.

That's why the Apostle Paul warns us in 1 Thessalonians 5:21, *"Test all things; hold fast what is good!"*

In order to accomplish this, you need to be part of a church that emphasizes teaching of the Bible in a pure, thorough, unaltered and uncompromised manner.

The more of God's word that you learn, the quicker you will recognize deception, and therefore, avoid its subtle trap!

Additional copies of:

The Christ Conspiracy

and other books by
Jack Michael

can be ordered from:

Jack Michael Outreach Ministries
P. O. Box 10688
Winston-Salem, N. C. 27108-0688

Other books include:

Deception in the End Times ($5.00)

The Best Way to Know God's Will ($3.00)